"Sweet ron
I want to visit Nestled h...... .... and over again!"

-ELANA JOHNSON
USA Today bestselling author of the *Hawthorn Harbor* series
and the *Getaway Bay* series

"Romance done right! Already looking forward to the next
Nestled Hollow love story. This series is going to be a keeper!"

-KIMBERLY KREY
Best-selling author of the *Sweet Montana Brides* series

COMING HOME TO THE TOP OF MAIN STREET

COMING HOME TO THE TOP OF MAIN STREET

A Nestled Hollow Romance Prequel

MEG EASTON

MOUNTAIN HEIGHTS
— PUBLISHING —

For Kyle

COMING HOME TO THE TOP OF MAIN STREET

A Nestled Hollow Romance

By Meg Easton

Chapter One
———————

*J*oselyn Zimmerman walked through the packed snow in Snowdrift Springs Park as the last of sunset faded away, looking at all the ice sculptures lit by brilliant colorful lights. She had forgotten how much she loved snuggling up in warm clothes, breathing the crisp mountain air, being surrounded by family, taking in all the beautiful ephemeral pieces of art. They had seen dragons, a couple dancing, a castle, a mountain lion, a person skiing, and her favorite, a family laughing together on a couch. All made of ice.

"It has been too long since I've been able to come to this," Joselyn said to her sister, Macie, who had her trusty big dogs Reese and Lola at her side, and her sister-in-law, Hannah. "I miss Nestled Hollow."

The Fire and Ice Festival was always in late January, which was usually too soon after Christmas for her to be able take work off again to visit Nestled Hollow. But this year, the financial software company she worked for had all hands on deck for the rolling out of their new app on January 1. And since they required them to be there on days they'd normally have off, they gave them some free days as compensation, and she jumped at the opportunity to come to the festival.

"I'm glad you could finally get the time off," Hannah said as she crouched down to put one-year-old Jason's mitten back on him for the tenth time, while her three-year-old Drew and Macie's dogs Reese and Lola attempted to be a little too helpful. "How has work been?"

Joselyn looked toward the next sculpture on the path around the park—the last one. "It's slowly killing off my creativity. I got my MBA so I could start my own business. Not so I could work for a huge corporation."

As they walked toward the sculpture, Macie said, "Why are you still there, then?"

"It's definitely the ridiculously good pay that's kept me from quitting. I figure if I can't be running my own business, I might as well be making the money I'm going to use to one day fund it." The spreadsheet in her brain sent out a wave of refreshing contentment every time she added some more to the Future Business Savings tab.

The last sculpture was of a campfire, the logs and fire cut completely out of ice, an orange flickering light at its base making the flames come alive. Next to the fire was a person sitting on a stump, bundled up in winter clothing, holding a marshmallow on a stick over the fire itself. A blue light shone on the camper, making the piece feel perfect for the Fire and Ice Festival.

"So why don't you just start your own business already?" Hannah asked. "You know all that you can possibly know without actually doing it. I'm pretty sure you have the spreadsheet to prove it."

"I know everything *except* what kind of business to have,"

Joselyn said as they stood around the ice campfire, admiring the way the artist had carved the flames in a way that looked so real, while being made out of a material that was virtually the exact opposite of fire. "I'm not like you two." She motioned at Hannah. "I didn't know I wanted to do cosmetology school right after graduation and be working on Main Street by the time I was nineteen. Or," she said, motioning at her sister Macie, "knowing I wanted to start Paws and Relax since I was seventeen."

Joselyn looked out across the sea of colored sculptures spread around the park. "Since I was first old enough to get a job at sixteen, I've worked every part time job imaginable, trying to figure out what business I want, and recording everything in my spreadsheet. I always figured that eventually the spreadsheet would lead the way. But it's been eleven years of working in small businesses and I'm no closer to an answer."

"Look, Momma!" Drew said, pulling on Hannah's coat sleeve, "That's where the hot chocolate and ice cream and Daddy is!"

Joselyn laughed as the three-year-old led them all toward the arches that, every year, towered over each of the two booths—one said "Fire" at the top, and had flames dancing up the sides of the arch, and the other said "Ice," and looked like interwoven icicles clung to it.

Under the Fire arch, Tory, who owned Love a Latte, the coffee shop in town, was serving a line of people. Her sign said the choices were spearmint hot chocolate and spiced apple cider. With as cold as it was outside, both sounded amazing.

But under the Ice arch, her brother and her brother's best friend, Marcus, caught her attention and she headed toward that booth.

"Daddy!" Drew shouted as he raced to Joselyn's brother,

Everett, who was standing next to Marcus behind the counter of the Ice booth. Everett picked Drew up and started showing him both ice cream flavors.

Joselyn watched Marcus as he scooped ice cream for the family at the front of the line, his broad shoulders and the muscles in those big strong arms flexing as he pressed the scoop against the hard ice cream in the bucket, an ever-present smile spread across his face. It had been more than a decade since they'd snuck behind almost everyone's back in high school and dated. When they broke up and he disappeared for two months, she had to act normally around her family, while nursing a broken heart worse than anything she'd experienced since.

But knowing they'd see each other every time her family got together and a million times in between when he was hanging out with one of her twin brothers, she and Marcus got past any feelings they had for each other and had agreed upon a truce years ago. With as great as he was looking now that he was in his late twenties, it was a good thing.

"The hot chocolate ice cream with salted caramel swirls and marshmallows is the obvious choice," Macie said as she looked at the sign on the booth, "but I don't know. That blue ice cream with the Oreos has me intrigued."

"I'm freezing," Hannah said as she gathered her toddler into her arms. "You two go ahead and be crazy with your frozen food when you're outside in the freezing cold. I'm going to get some of Tory's nice warm spiced apple cider."

When it was Joselyn's and Macie's turn at the front of the line, Marcus greeted them with a smile that looked like he was thrilled to see them. It was how the man greeted every living thing, but it still made her smile.

"Ladies! Lovely to see you today! The spicy hot ice cream, or keeping it cool?"

"I see you're keeping it cool," Joselyn said. "Forgot your coat again?"

Marcus's booming laugh sounded across the park. He held up one an arm like he was showing off a biceps and said, "Remember? I've got lava instead of bone marrow."

"But you better not let my mom see you out here without a coat," Macie said. "You know what she'll say."

Everett laughed this time. He nodded his head toward a wagon at the edge of the booth. "He brought a coat—he put it on as soon as he saw her coming."

Marcus nodded. "She was in line with a crowd, too, so I had to keep it on for a good fifteen minutes. I nearly burst into flames before I could take it off again."

Joselyn chuckled and peered over the edge of the container to see the hot chocolate one. "Well, I think I have ice in my bone marrow and I'm interested to see how spicy works with ice cream, so give me the hot stuff."

"I'll keep it cool," Macie said.

As Marcus was scooping their ice cream, he made eye contact with Joselyn briefly. "I haven't seen you for a while."

"I know. We missed you at Thanksgiving and Christmas—it's strange when you're not at family things."

"One of the perils of being a chef," Marcus said as he handed Macie her ice cream cone, "is working pretty much every holiday, weekend, and evening. I managed to make it here for New Year's, though." He went to work scooping Joselyn's next.

"And I was working then. I hadn't heard that you were going to be here for the Fire and Ice Festival."

"I made a quart of each flavor and paid the Keetch's a visit."

He winked. "Sweetened them up enough to ask me to come, and here I am. I hadn't heard you were going to be here."

She had decided that she had worked in a home appliance shop long enough to know that it wasn't a business she ever wanted to run, so she had quit and had her last day earlier in the week. She wasn't even going to start looking for her next part-time job until Monday. Maybe she would try for a board game shop. She hadn't worked in one of those before. "It was one of those rare moments when I unexpectedly had time off at both the day job and the night job, so I jumped in my car and came straight here."

"Well, it's good to see you both." He handed Joselyn her ice cream cone, then turned to Macie. "And I heard you're finally going to open Paws and Relax."

Macie grinned. "When the current building lease is up, so five more months."

As Macie told Marcus all about her plans, Joselyn wished she could talk about her future plans with as much confidence as her sister could—her sister who was almost two years younger than her. Instead, she felt like she was just standing on the shore of life, convinced that one day she was going to dive in and live it to the fullest, but was currently still standing there, trying to decide on a plan to eventually at least stick a toe into the water.

When a family stepped behind them in line at the same time Hannah joined them again at the Ice booth, cup of warm cider in hand, her husband Everett said, "Why don't you leave the kids with me while you three go catch up. I'll meet you back at my parents' after."

Jason toddled over to his dad, and Hannah gave Everett a grin, a kiss, and said, "Thanks!"

Someday, when Joselyn did finally dive in and create her

ideal life, she was going to have that, too. A husband who would look at her the way her brother just looked at Hannah, and kids who were as adorable as Drew and Jason. But long before she could do that, she needed to get the rest of her life figured out.

"Come on," Hannah said, grabbing Joselyn's free hand and leading her to the pathway in the snow leading out of the park. "We're going to go take a walk down Main Street."

Macie, of course, seemed to love the idea and couldn't get enough of seeing the site of her future business. As thrilled as Joselyn was that things were working out for her sister, it also made her realize even more deeply how much her own life wasn't working out so well. But Macie was family, so of course she walked with them to show support.

"Mmm," Macie moaned as she ate her ice cream. "This is amazing."

As they walked, Joselyn took a bite of hers, too. The silky sweet chocolate melted on her tongue, creamy and smooth, the salt from the caramel making an incredible contrast to the sweet creaminess of the chocolate, so much flavor bursting through that she felt like she couldn't even take it all in. As soon as she swallowed, the spicy heat from the "hot" part of the hot chocolate ice cream spread across her mouth, the most interesting sensation to be paired with a frozen treat. She had never experienced such a depth of flavor coming from a single bite before. She quickly took another bite to experience the flavor even more fully. "I never knew ice cream could be this good. I'm so sorry you didn't get any, Hannah. Want a bite of mine?"

Hanna laughed as they walked down the slight hill to the road. "Marcus is staying at our house, so I already got the preview in my nice, warm home. I'll stick with the warm drink out here." She took a sip of her cider.

"I'm so jealous that you have this stuff in your home," Macie said around a bite of her ice cream.

Joselyn's mouth was so cold from the ice cream that her puffs of breath were no longer visible in the cold air. She could use Marcus's lava for bone marrow right now. She was close to shivering but didn't want to stop eating. She took another bite of hers as Hannah turned to her and asked, "So why haven't you and Marcus ever dated?"

Joselyn nearly choked on the melting chocolate. "Hannah!" She swallowed the bite she'd taken. "He's practically my brother!"

"But he's *not* your brother. He's just your brother's best friend."

"My family claimed him as one of our own when he was nine. He used to play practical jokes on us all the time. I was the annoying little sister." All the things she used to repeat over and over back when she had to in order to keep her mind off him. She didn't have to anymore—not unless someone suggested something as crazy as the two of them dating.

"Maybe back then. Not so much now. You can't deny that there's chemistry between you two—it's one of the first things I noticed when I started dating your brother."

Macie shook her head as they turned at the corner by Back Porch Grill onto Main Street. "I can't believe you're married to Everett and you're saying this."

Hannah cocked her head to the side, clearly not understanding.

Macie glanced at Hannah. "Have you ever mentioned to Everett that you thought Marcus and Joselyn should date?"

"Yeah. He said he thinks you two would never work out. But I think he's wrong."

"No, he's right," Joselyn said. She knew that firsthand, even if everyone else didn't. "And that's exactly why, back when we were in middle school, he and Kennon made me and Marcus both cross-our-hearts-and-hope-to-die, pinkie swear, spit-handshake promise that we would never date."

"Why? Why would they do that?"

"Because if the two of them dated and then broke up," Macie said, "can you imagine how awkward family get-togethers would be after that?"

Joselyn didn't have to imagine it. She had experienced exactly that after their three month long secret relationship ended during her sophomore year in high school.

"Oh," Hannah said. "They're afraid it could make Marcus feel unwelcome in the family."

"Right," Joselyn said as they crossed Center Street onto the top half of Main Street. "Besides, I need to get my own life together before I can add someone else. And I am far from being there." She took another bite of her ice cream.

"That's actually why I wanted to come down here." Hannah threw her cup into a garbage can in front of Best Dressed, and then started walking with more purpose toward the top of Main Street.

Joselyn glanced at Macie, but Macie just shrugged and the two of them finished their ice cream cones as they followed Hannah.

Hannah led them over the pedestrian bridge that crossed Snowdrift Springs, the creek that ran down the middle of Main Street. Then she stopped in front of the building that, in five months from now, would be Macie's new business where people could hang out with pets when they couldn't have any of their own. "Okay," Hannah said, putting her hands on Macie's shoulders and positioning her front and center, facing the building. "Here we've got the future home of Paws and Relax, with its cute little side yard where the animals can play."

Hannah paused for a moment as they all looked at the building, then she put her hands on Joselyn's shoulders and led her to the building next door, the one at the very top of Main Street. Just like she had with Macie, Hannah led Joselyn to the front center and squared her shoulders so she was facing the building. Joselyn looked at Larry's Hardware, not understanding at all what Hannah was doing as Hannah stood, hands on her hips, a pleased look on her face. "And I believe that this should be the future home of the business that you are going to open."

"The hardware store is closing?"

Hannah nodded. "He's closing shop and leasing the building out in two months. Larry says that he's ready to retire, and that there just hasn't been enough business to justify selling it, so he thought the place should retire with him."

Macie hurried from her building to Joselyn and grabbed her hands. "You should do it! Then we can open businesses together and brainstorm and make mistakes and figure out what to do together. The apartment I signed a lease on here is opening up in two months. There's two bedrooms—you can move in with me."

"But what kind of business would I open? I haven't even figured that part out yet."

"We'll help you brainstorm," Hannah said.

"We will. You have that giant spreadsheet with all the places you've worked since you turned sixteen. We can look through that."

"And I can tell you which ones are businesses that I've heard people in town saying that they wish Nestled Hollow had."

Joselyn stared at the hardware store, picturing what it might look like as a business she was running. She imagined what it would feel like to own that business. To look at this building with pride, knowing that she had created the business it housed, and excitement bubbled up inside her. Could it finally be her time? She had stood there on life's shore in her swimsuit for so long, trying to find the perfect spot to jump in. Could this be it? Did the perfect situation really just open up to her?

Goosebumps covered her arms and a thrill raced up her spine. She had graduated second in her class with a business degree. She had a good day job that had allowed her to save enough to open this business. She had worked at forty different night jobs at small businesses over the past ten and a half years so she would know what she wanted and how to best manage it.

And now, for the first time, she saw a path to exactly what she wanted right before her.

She turned to her sister and her sister-in-law, a lightness in her chest practically lifting her off the ground. "It's perfect. I want to do it. Let's call Larry, then head back to my parents, and we can all brainstorm."

Chapter Two

---

*M*arcus was handing the last ice cream cone to a family of four when the elderly Mr. and Mrs. Keetch walked up, arm-in-arm, right between his booth and Love a Latte's.

"Looks like that might be the last family to leave the sculptures," Linda Keetch said, "so you two are probably good to clean up."

Marcus tossed the ice cream scoop into the bucket of warm water. "Whew! Because I was down to scraping my last bucket on both flavors."

"I've run all the way out of hot chocolate," Tory said, "and I'm close on apple cider."

Ed Keetch nodded. "Well, that's what happens when you provide the best there is. I don't think we've ever heard so many positive comments on the Fire and Ice treats in all the years we've held it."

As the older couple walked away, Marcus looked at the empty cartons of ice cream. He had made what he thought was more than he could even come close to giving out, and it had been a good thing. He grinned at Everett. "This was fun. I'm glad I did it."

"It seems like everyone in Nestled Hollow is glad you did, too," Everett said. "Do you make these flavors for your restaurant?"

Marcus shook his head. "I wish. I've tried to talk them into it—their ice cream machine is the best I've ever worked with —but all they want on the menu is vanilla. Now don't get me wrong. I make the best vanilla there is. But it's still *vanilla*."

"Have they *tried* your other flavors?" Everett said, with a note of disbelief in his voice that made Marcus smile.

"Yep."

Everett shook his head. "You're a resource they've been wasting."

"My ice cream was yummy!" Everett's three-year-old son Drew said as he rubbed his stomach.

Marcus crouched down and tickled Drew. "It wasn't too cold for you on this super cold day?"

The little boy grabbed his stomach and laughed in a way that made Marcus laugh, too. "It wasn't too cold for me because I have super powers. I can even fly."

"You can?"

Drew nodded. "Want to see?" When Marcus nodded, the little boy leaned forward and whispered, "I need your help."

So Marcus picked him up and held him above his head, flying him around the little booth, and Everett picked up little Jason and joined him, before sitting them both down again.

Everett looked down at his sons, who both were grinning, then he turned his attention to Marcus. "Out of the two of us, I always figured you'd be the first to settle down with a wife and have a couple kids."

Marcus turned to his ice cream buckets and started

stacking them into the wagon he'd pulled all his ice cream and supplies to the booth in. "Me, too." His mind immediately flashed to his 12th grade English class. Mrs. G had them write down where they were going to be ten years from then, and he wrote that he'd be married and have a bunch of little kids. It was not long before graduation, so he'd been eighteen. So it had been about ten and a half years from when he'd written that prediction.

"You haven't mentioned dating anyone seriously for a while."

Marcus dumped the water he'd had his ice cream scoops sitting in into the snow, and then put the scoops and the container into the wagon. "That's because I have no life. I wish someone would've warned me back when I decided to be a chef that it would mean working mostly nights, weekends, and holidays. It's sucking the soul out of me." He didn't really meet people to date at work, either. Everything about it had been wearing on him for quite a while, and he had been trying to figure out what he should do about it.

Everett's younger son put his arms in the air and said, "Hold you?" so Everett picked him up.

"You look like you already have an idea of what to do about that."

Marcus shrugged. "All I know is I can't keep going like I have. This isn't what I want my life to be. I became a chef because food brings families together, and to honor the memory of my mama. But what it's really doing," he said as he added the stack of remaining cones and the stack of cups to the cart, "is keeping me from having my own family."

He picked up the handle to the cart and started pulling it through the pathway shoveled free of snow, Everett and Jason beside him, Drew skipping ahead of them.

"You still get time off work, though," Everett said. "Why aren't you dating anyone?"

"You know how important family is to me. I haven't found someone who feels the same way." That wasn't entirely true—he had found someone who felt exactly the same way as him, and he'd been in love with her since his senior year of high school. But he couldn't exactly say "Because I haven't ever found someone that I love as much as I love your sister and probably never will" to his best friend. And it wasn't for lack of looking, either. But he'd gotten to the point that he was ready to give up.

Everett popped the hatch of his compact SUV and Marcus lifted the wagon and adjusted it to fit in the space.

"Keep looking," Everett said. "You'll find her."

"Actually," Marcus said, eyeing his friend, dreading saying his next words because he knew Everett would hate hearing them, "I'm thinking of moving back to Hawaii."

"What?" Everett boomed as he slammed down the trunk.

"Now that Nana is gone and my cousins moved out of state, there's not so much for me here. I haven't been back since my grandparents took me and my cousins in when I was eleven, but I have a lot of family there. I need family, Everett."

He thought Everett would tell him that he *did* have family here, and honestly, he probably wouldn't have survived his teenage years without the Zimmermans. He very much considered them family, and they were the one thing that had kept him from packing up and moving to Hawaii before today. But he was standing on the sidelines watching the Zimmerman family grow, and the need to have his own family grow was strong. If he moved, maybe he would finally get over Joselyn and be able to find someone he could imagine having a life with.

15

But instead of trying to convince Marcus that the Zimmermans were all the family he needed, Everett just studied him for a few moments. Then he said, "Hop in. I want to show you something."

Marcus buckled in Drew while Everett buckled in Jason, then he got into the passenger's seat, his mind going through possibilities of what Everett wanted to show him. Something at the Zimmerman home that he spent so many hours in growing up? Something at Everett's house?

But when Everett pulled out of the parking lot, instead of turning left, toward the big square of land where his parents, he and Hannah, and three of his six siblings had built homes, Everett turned right, and then on to Main Street. As they drove toward the top of Main, Marcus looked out at each of the buildings. It never mattered how long it had been since he had last visited Nestled Hollow; Main Street always made him feel like he was coming home.

When they got to the very top, Everett pulled into a parking spot right in front of the hardware store and turned off his engine but left his headlights on.

"Why are we stopping here, Daddy?" Drew asked.

"We're just doing to talk for a minute. Can you do me a huge favor and tell your brother a story so he won't get bored?"

As Drew's voice changed to a three-year-old's storytelling cadence from the backseat, Everett said, "Which makes you happier: cooking food or making ice cream?"

Marcus thought about it for a moment. His first reaction had been to say ice cream, but that could've been because he didn't get as many chances to make it. The more he thought about how he felt as he was making menu items for the restaurant and how he felt when he was coming up with a new ice cream flavor, the answer became obvious. "Ice cream."

Everett nodded, and then thought for a moment. "Okay. Now, if you couldn't be a chef at your restaurant but had to pick another job there and still got paid the same amount, what would it be?"

Marcus didn't even have to stop to think this time. "Waiter. I hate that I don't get a chance to interact with the customers when I'm in the kitchen."

"So what I'm hearing is that you have a job that is sucking the soul out of you, and you need more chances to be around people. Have you ever thought of opening your own ice cream shop?"

"Nope."

"Why not?"

"Because I don't know how to do that."

"You're a smart guy. You could figure it out. You practically just did market research right here in Nestled Hollow and found out that you'd have a very enthusiastic customer base. Tourists love ice cream, and we get plenty of those here. An ice cream shop is something Nestled Hollow has been lacking."

Marcus just stared at his friend. Having his own shop wasn't something he had ever considered. He had seen the work it took to keep the restaurant running and was always glad none of that fell on his shoulders. But as much as he hadn't ever been interested in exploring something like this before, the idea excited him like nothing else had in a while. Running an ice cream shop would be much more of a daytime thing than his current job was. "And do it where? It's not like Nestled Hollow is flooded with empty buildings, just waiting for an ice cream shop to move in."

A smile spread across Everett's face, then he spread his hands wide toward the building that his lights landed on. "Hannah told me earlier today that Larry is retiring and closing the hardware shop. It'll be available to rent in two months. You can spend another month after that in construction and be open in three. That'd be plenty of time to get everything worked out."

"You think it would?"

Everett nodded. "Totally."

Marcus got out of the vehicle and walked up to the closed hardware store. He had been in the store a few times over the years, but he had never looked at the place as though he would one day turn it into an ice cream shop, until now. Dim lights were on in the store, but the bulk of the light came from Everett's headlights behind him. He cupped his hands at the sides of his face and pressed against the glass, looking inside, imagining what it would be like to not have all the shelves of building supplies and instead have tables, chairs, and a counter to order ice cream with a case of his own unique flavors inside.

When he had decided to go to culinary school, the feeling he was experiencing right now was exactly what he had been hoping for. Never had he imagined that an ice cream shop would be the thing to give it to him, though. But it felt right. Exciting. Full of possibilities. And with the different schedule it would require, maybe it would even lead him to a place where he could one day get married and have a family of his own.

He heard Everett get out of the car behind him, but he still kept looking, unable to take his eyes off this perfect dream that he'd never even thought of before now. Everett clapped him on the back. "What do you think?"

Marcus knew exactly how off-limits Joselyn was. If she still lived in Nestled Hollow, it would be a solid no. He wouldn't be able to stand seeing her so often and knowing they could never be together. But she lived in Denver just like he did now, so his heart would actually be safer being here than in the same city as her. Not that he ever saw here there—Denver was a big place. And the Zimmermans had always been family. Not all of the Zimmerman clan still lived in Nestled Hollow, but the oldest four had come back and built homes on the family plot. Being around them again might just give him the family he was craving.

As long as Joselyn didn't move back before he found a way to get over her and found someone else just like her that he could marry, everything would work out exactly right.

"I think it's perfect."

He could hear the smile in Everett's voice when he said, "My mom just texted—dinner should be ready in fifteen minutes. How about we head over and let my family hear the good news?"

Chapter Three

*J*oselyn chopped vegetables for the salad in her mom's kitchen, surrounded by family members, her laptop on the counter with her spreadsheet open.

"What about a laundromat?" Hannah asked. "I know that All Nestled Inn has one, but it would be nice to have one that isn't also used for hotel linens."

It didn't feel right, though. "It would take a lot of work to get plumbing and electrical wired, and then to get all the equipment, but what about after it gets going? It wouldn't take much at all to run it. I think I would get bored too quickly."

"Yeah," her dad said from where he was helping her niece and nephew set the table. "It would be a shame to spend all that knowledge and experience you've gained on something so small."

"How about a bookstore?" her sister Nicole asked. "You liked working at Bookies while you were in college."

Joselyn nodded, stopped cutting the cucumber she was on,

and clicked on the tab in her spreadsheet for the bookstore. "It was a lot of fun."

Her mom shook her head. "I don't know, though. Our library here is used so much—I'm not sure there's enough people in town who would change their habits and switch to a bookstore."

"That's true," Joselyn said. It might not even be worth doing market research for that. They'd been talking about building a bigger library for quite a while because of how many books were constantly being checked out. This town really loved their library.

"A flower shop?" Macie asked. "Then people wouldn't have to go to Mountain Springs for corsages and boutonnieres for school dances."

"That sounds like a lot of fun. I'll add it to the list." She clicked back to the tab where they were putting suggestions and added it before going back to chopping veggies.

"Hey," her brother Zach said from across the great room where he was on the floor playing with his little kids, "you should do one of those spas with a massage therapist! Lia is always saying she wishes she could have a spa day."

"That's a really great idea," Joselyn said, pointing the knife she was holding his direction. "Especially since we get so many tourists." She added it to her list. It was probably a really good idea, but in the nearly forty places she had worked side jobs at, a spa was never one of them, so she didn't have any spa-specific knowledge.

She was just clicking save again on the file when she heard the front door open and Marcus's booming voice call out "Hello, Zimmermans!" like he had done since he was nine and a half and first claimed her family as his own. Her nephews ran into the great room, and her brother and Marcus followed closely behind.

"Guess who is going to open an ice cream shop on Main Street?" Everett said, then clapped Marcus on the shoulder. "This guy!"

Joselyn's confusion was echoed by everyone in the room, then after a short pause, Hannah squeaked out, "In the hardware store building?"

"Yep!" Both Everett and Marcus were grinning ear-to-ear, and Joselyn's stomach fell. "It was perfect timing that you told me today."

"Larry already told you that you got the building?" Hannah looked between her husband and Marcus and then to Joselyn.

"No," Marcus said. "It's not a done deal like Everett's making it sound. I called Larry on the way here and told him I wanted the building. He said he had one other offer, and that he was going to decide next week."

"But," Everett said, dragging out the word, "Larry couldn't stop talking about how incredible Marcus's ice cream was at the Fire and Ice Festival, so I'm betting he'll choose Marcus over the other guy. Isn't that fantastic? Why are you all not showing more excitement?"

Joselyn was having a hard time keeping her emotions in check. She had gone through way too big of a range of them today to deal with this news after being so excited about her own possibilities for the building.

"Because the 'other guy,'" Hannah said, "is Joselyn. I showed her the building right after we left the festival."

"Oh," Everett said. "That's bad."

"No, maybe it's perfect," her mom said, smiling broadly like everything was somehow going to work out. She turned toward Joselyn. "You've been looking for the perfect business, and it looks like you found it! You and Marcus can just team up."

"No!" Joselyn said at the same time that Marcus, Everett, and her dad said the same thing.

Marcus met Joselyn's eyes, and it was clear that the thought horrified him just as much as it had her. She was surprised at the intensity of her dad's "no," though. Everett and her dad were both looking at the floor, and everyone else in her big family was looking at each other with awkwardness, confusion, or pity on their faces.

Joselyn set her knife on the counter, shut her laptop, took off her apron and laid it over the back of a chair, and headed out onto the back patio. She hadn't even taken time to grab her coat, and she sucked in a gasp as the cold air bit into her. Wrapping her arms around herself, she looked out toward Oliver's, Zach's, Nichole's, and Everett's homes, and over the deep snow that covered the field that would one day be hold hers, Kennon's, and Macie's homes. It wasn't a big deal to not lease that building on Main Street. Sure, it had excited her more so than she had been excited about anything in a long time. But yesterday she hadn't even known about the possibility and she had been just fine.

Bored, stuck in a life that wasn't moving, and feeling vast amounts of potential built up inside of her that she couldn't seem to tap into, but fine nonetheless. She could go back to that state again and be okay.

The door opened behind her, and the warmth from the house touched her backside for a fleeting moment before she heard the door close. Macie stepped up next to her and held out her coat.

"Thanks," she said, slipping her arms into the sleeves and crossing her arms in front of her again to help hold in the heat.

Macie zipped her own coat and put her hands in her pockets, looking out across the field with Joselyn.

Joselyn didn't want to turn to look inside the house in case all eyes were on her, but she was curious. "What's going on inside?"

Macie lifted a shoulder in a shrug. "Mom and Hannah are leading the charge that you two should work together, and Everett and Dad, surprisingly, are saying what a bad idea it is, and how much potential it would have to cause a rift in the family."

"And Marcus?"

"He wanted to come out here and tell you that you could have the shop. Me and Nicole asked him to wait—you both need some time to think."

"I'm going to tell him that he should have the shop."

Joselyn let out a quick breath, almost in a huff. "You're doing the same thing he is. You both should be talking through this."

"Okay," Joselyn said, turning to face Macie and leaning her hip against the railing, "I'll talk through it. I haven't decided on a business. Marcus has. His business idea is a great one, too—I mean you've tried his ice cream. All he has to do is sell ice cream like that, and his shop will be an instant hit. He's leagues ahead of where I'm at. I'm still unsure about everything."

"I saw you look at that building, though," Macie said. "You want it."

"Sure I do. But it won't be the last building to open up in Nestled Hollow."

"The next one might be *years* away. Could be a decade."

"Well, maybe by then I'll have everything figured out and finally know what I want to do." Instead of being ready to jump in life's lake, she suddenly felt like she was backing away. Alarmingly fast and far.

"And there's no chance you'll just partner with Marcus?"

Joselyn let out a huff of breath in a humorless chuckle. Macie was the only person in the family who knew that she and Marcus had secretly dated while they were in high school. Although Joselyn and Marcus were both worried that Everett and Kennon suspected it, they were pretty sure the twins never found out. "Maybe you don't remember how awkward things were when we broke up."

"Oh, I remember. I was fourteen and boy crazy and was watching you like a hawk to learn all I could about dating so I would be a pro by the time I finally got to be sixteen and could date. I hadn't experienced anything like it myself so I didn't have the same understanding, but I saw how miserable you were."

Joselyn looked back out across the snow. "We only dated for a few months, but that was my first breakup, and it hurt." Plus, it was Marcus. That had made it so much more difficult than any old first breakup. And then, after being such a staple in their family's lives, he had just stepped out of their lives for two months. He never came over to the house, and somehow managed to never be where she was at school. That had made the breakup so much worse.

"And then once he started coming to family things again, seeing him at our house constantly was so hard for both of us, yet neither of us could do anything different or Everett and Kennon would know that we broke our promise and dated anyway."

"But being business partners isn't the same as dating each other."

Joselyn shook her head. "You're right. It isn't. But what if we found out we couldn't actually work together? What if it went disastrously? Do you remember Cade Rowley and Flora Erekson? They were in my grade."

Macie nodded.

"They were inseparable in high school—the best of friends. They had a dream of running a business together, and right after college, they opened a sandwich shop in Littleton. They had different opinions on how to do things, and the business ended up failing. They didn't go back to being friends after. Two decades of friendship was lost, all because they went into business together."

"That doesn't mean that you and Marcus wouldn't be able to work together."

Joselyn shook her head. "I've been studying how to run my own business for a really long time. I know exactly how I want to do things, and I'm pretty sure I'll be headstrong about it. If Marcus didn't agree, we could end up just like Cade and Flora. Then I don't think either of us would want to be around each other at family things. And you know how wrong it feels not to have him at family things. I couldn't be the cause of that."

"I totally get that." Macie reached out and placed a hand on the top of her arm and stayed silent for a moment before asking, "You're sure you're willing to give up the building?"

The truth was, she felt a sharp pain stabbing her heart. The part of her that had lain large and dormant that had zinged to life when she looked at the hardware shop and thought of it being her building now felt like it was dying off, not that it was just returning to dormancy.

But what was the alternative? She really had three options. She could partner with Marcus, which had the potential to cause forever damage to her very large family. Or she could demand that he step back and let her have the building, especially since she put in the offer to lease it first. But the guilt associated with that might haunt her forever. If whatever business she chose didn't work out, or went through hard times, or wasn't exactly what the town needed, she would wonder how well the ice cream shop would've done if she had let Marcus have his chance. Could she enjoy her business with that constant wonder hanging over her?

Or she could let Marcus have his chance with the building, lick her wounds, and then regroup and come up with a new plan and when the time was right, move forward with absolute confidence.

Really, out of three less-than-perfect options, giving him the chance at the building was the best one. She nodded. "I'm sure I'm willing. The next time a building comes up, I'll be ready for it."

Macie studied her for several long moments, then nodded.

Joselyn finally turned toward the house, and saw that every family member present who was over the age of four sat somewhere in the great room, watching her go through the decision-making process. But her eyes fell on Marcus's. His face was full of uncertainty and worry and apprehension and he got to his feet, hesitating, as if unsure whether it was now okay to approach her about a solution yet or not.

She could do this. She told herself that karma would have her back, and she went inside to let Marcus know that she would move forward with her dream in a different way, and that he should move forward with his as planned.

Chapter Four

"*H*ey, my man!" Marcus said as Dustin came into the kitchens at Kleinman Terrace. "Good to see you! How are you?"

Dustin laughed. "I had one of those days where you can't seem to do anything right. Want to know why I didn't just call in sick and go back to bed? Because you're always so happy to see me." He bumped Marcus's shoulder as he walked past—their usual greeting, since at least one of them usually had either freshly-washed hands, or hands in the middle of food prep.

"It's 'cause you're always such a ray of sunshine," Marcus said as he cut some fish into fillets. "And come on—we both know it was thoughts of how 'cool' you'd feel doing the Wednesday organizing of the walk-in fridge that brought you here."

"Let's just say it was a tie."

Dustin grabbed an apron, then disappeared to the backside of the walk-in. Marcus chuckled and placed the rest of the prepared fish in the metal pan, washed his hands, then covered the pan with plastic wrap and put it in the front of the walk-in. Prepping for the dinner rush was the slowest part of the day for Marcus. The part where he had too much time to think.

It had been eleven days since Everett had first planted the idea of Marcus opening his own ice cream shop. Nine days since Larry had called and told him that Joselyn had pulled her name out of consideration and that he was accepting Marcus's offer. And eight days since the excitement at opening his own shop fled and fear and worry took its place.

As he got out the beef tenderloin to cut it into serving-sized pieces, he wondered if, over the past eleven days, Joselyn had experienced just as many second thoughts at pulling her name out of the running for the building as he had at keeping his name in. He knew absolutely nothing about running a business. The brothers who owned Kleinman's weren't exactly the kinds of guys that he could go to for advice, either. They weren't going to be happy when they found out his plans to open his own shop and quit in two and a half months.

He cut another slice of beef. The whole thing was so overwhelming, and he didn't even know where to start. Thoughts kept popping in his head of things that would need to be done before opening a shop, but he had no idea what order they should be done in, and what steps were most important to happen first. Or what steps he didn't even know he was missing. Why did he think he could do this with no experience under his belt?

After finishing prepping the steaks, he washed his hands, then went to the back counter and picked up his cell phone, turning it around in his hands. He had picked up his phone dozens of times a day over the previous eight days, warring with himself about whether or not he should ask Joselyn for help. He had known her since he was nine and she was seven, so he knew how long she'd had the dream to open her own business. And after giving up her chance at making her dream come true so that he could, he figured the last thing she wanted was a call from him asking for help.

But he didn't know anyone else he could call. Or anyone more brilliant. Or more beautiful. Or more perfect.

Asking for her help was a bad idea. An incredibly bad idea. He needed to work closely with someone to figure all this stuff out, and he didn't think his heart could handle it being Joselyn. Maybe there were companies out there who helped people set up businesses. Or freelance people who did that. He had no idea. If there were, he didn't even know enough to know how to find them. Or how expensive they would be. There were probably a million things about running a business that he didn't even know that he didn't know yet.

And the clock just kept ticking.

Three months didn't seem like a very long time to get a brand new business up and running, especially when no prep work had been done ahead of time. He had already wasted eight days, and he was no closer to knowing what to do. How many more days could he waste just trying to get over his reluctance to ask Joselyn for help?

Text.

That's what he needed to do. If he texted her to ask for help, then he wouldn't be putting her on the spot to answer immediately. She could see the text, take as long as she needed to think about her answer, and then let her anger at the audacity of him asking fizzle a bit before she responded. Or she could just let the anger spill out immediately in a text— whichever she wanted.

Before he could get a chance to talk himself out of asking,

he opened the texting app, brought up Joselyn's name, then typed in, *Hi, Jos. Have I told you lately how amazing you are? And how much I appreciate you?*

That was exactly how he felt, and he wanted her to know that. But did it sound insincere, like he was just trying to butter her up? He deleted it. He would just have to tell her in person the next time he saw her, where she could see that he was sincere. Maybe just being direct would work best.

Hi, Jos. I don't know how to get a business started. I realize that helping me can't be at the top of your "things that would be fun" list, but do you think you could maybe point me in the right direction?

His finger hovered over the *send* icon for a moment, then he made himself just quickly push it. He was still staring at the screen, wondering if it had been a terrible idea when the little "Delivered" notification below the text changed to "Read." He couldn't stay here, hoping to get a response when it might not come for a while. So he put the phone back on the counter, pulled some food-prep gloves onto his hands, and went into the walk-in fridge to get a few whole chickens. Breaking them down not only made enough noise that he couldn't hear the buzz of a text, but it gave him a location to aim his nervous energy.

He stood at the meat counter with the cleaver, the repetitive motions of positioning the chicken, then the big swing and the thunk of the cleaver hitting the cutting board blocking out everything else.

Yet, somehow, he still heard the faint buzz of his phone from the back counter. He froze, telling himself he should just wait until the end of the night to look. Or at least until he was done with prep. Or with this one chicken.

He didn't manage to do any of that, though. He pulled the gloves off and tossed them in the trash, washed his hands, then went to the back counter and picked up his phone. The message *I'm free at 8* stared back at him.

He couldn't believe it. She was willing!

Except he would still be working at eight. She was helping him, though, and he was willing to take that help whenever she wanted to give it. He could just take his break then. Maybe he'd whip her up a great meal and they could eat while they talked. Like a peace offering.

I'm at Kleinman's. Do you mind coming here? I will make you a meal worth the drive.

This time he did stick around, staring at his phone.

8 it is.

Between both texts, she had used a total of seven words. With so few, he had no way to guess what she was thinking or how she was feeling about his request. He looked up at the clock. Another three and a half hours and he would find out.

The restaurant had been busy for a Wednesday night. The biggest rush, though, had hit just before six, and all five chefs in the kitchen had been running nonstop trying to keep up. It was finally slowing down in the lobby, though, so Marcus went to work making a meal for him and Joselyn. He didn't pull a plate straight from the menu, but instead chose items he thought she would like, based on the nineteen years he had known her, the last eleven or so of which he had been paying much closer attention than the first eight.

He placed the chicken club roulades on the plates first, arranging them so the asparagus poking out from the ends were perfectly arranged. Then he plated the roasted, caramelized cinnamon butternut squash, and then the perfectly browned crispy maple mustard stuffed potato balls.

He put a lot of care into the presentation of every dish that left his kitchen, but as he put the finishing touches on these two, he took even greater care. Even though he had known her for considerably longer now than he had back when he was a senior in high school and Joselyn was a sophomore, he was even more nervous about tonight than he had been about sneaking away from a school football game and meeting at his car before heading up the mountain for a picnic on their first date.

In the first true break in orders they'd had all night, Dustin walked over and leaned against the counter top Marcus was working on. "You've seemed uncharacteristically anxious for the past week. What's up?"

Marcus glanced at his friend. Had it been that obvious? With the way his bosses were, he really didn't want word to get out that he would be leaving. "It's nothing."

"You're especially anxious right now." He looked at the dishes he was finishing. "And wow, those are beautifully plated." Dustin glanced from the plates to the clock on the wall to Marcus, and understanding lit his face. "Ahh, I see. Your eight o'clock break is with a girl."

Marcus tried to keep his expression neutral so Dustin wouldn't be able to read anything into it. But he did anyway.

A smile spread across his face. "It's with a girl you really like. That one back home that you talk about in a very 'she's like a sister' way, but secretly you've been pining over for as long as I've known you."

Marcus's eyes darted to Dustin's in alarm.

The sous chef laughed loudly enough that it bounced off all the stainless steel surfaces in the kitchen. "Seeing this totally made coming in to work worth it today." Then he nodded toward the lobby. "Is that her?"

Marcus's gaze jerked toward the hostess podium where Avenlie was greeting Joselyn, and motioning her to walk with her to the table Marcus had asked her to reserve for them. He took off his apron and chef's hat and smock, washed his hands and arms, dried them with paper towels, and then ran the paper towels over his face. He ran his hands through his hair, straightened the front of his shirt, then took a deep breath before grabbing both plates and heading to the front to join Joselyn.

Chapter Five

$\mathcal{J}$oselyn would be lying if she'd said the past week and a half had been easy. She had questioned her decision to walk away from leasing Larry's building over and over. Some of the time she knew without a doubt that the choice she had made had been the right one. Some of the time that decision had just hurt her heart—it had been difficult to let go of the dream. The specific dream of a shop in that particular building hadn't been hers for long, but the general dream of owning a shop on Main Street had been with her since she was young.

And some of the time, she wondered if the reason why she had walked away was because of fear. She had been working toward running her own business for so long and had been planning and imagining what it would be like in all of her free time. When it finally become close to a reality, did she back away because she was afraid? Was she afraid of failing? Was she afraid of succeeding? She wasn't sure. In all her prep over the years, she hadn't prepared for this.

There was also the realization that she wanted Marcus to

have the shop because she cared about him and wanted him to be happy. And not in the same way she cared for her siblings and wanted them to be happy. She hadn't realized that she had residual feelings for Marcus from when they dated in high school. Or maybe these weren't from leftover from high school. Maybe this was new. The thought alarmed her and made her want to turn and run the other way.

But that realization was also why she had agreed to meet with Marcus when he had texted. And now here she sat, in his restaurant, her stomach a strange mix of emotions bubbling up that she couldn't quite name. She had known that he worked at this restaurant, but it was a good thirty minute drive from where she worked, and she just hadn't been here before. It was a nice restaurant, though. The tablecloths and table linens were nice, the waiters and waitresses were dressed impeccably, the lighting was low, and the decorations were modern, sparse, and expensive-looking.

Marcus walked through the swinging doors that led into the back, holding a plate of food in each hand, a smile spread across his face. She couldn't help but smile herself.

"Hi," she said as he neared, still not entirely sure if she was happy about being here, despite the smile on her face.

"Hello, Sunshine," he said, placing one of the plates in front of her and one in front of the chair opposite her. "Thank you for coming."

She was about to make a teasing comment about the time when she was ten and he was twelve and she won the bet about who could do more chin-ups and he had to cook her lunch. He had brought two plates to the kitchen table, one in each hand, just like now, and set one down in front of her like it was a fancy meal, but it was the most burnt, inedible grilled cheese she'd ever had. But when he set this plate in front of her, all she managed to say was "Wow!" She turned her plate so she could see it from all angles. "This is a piece of art made out of food!"

Marcus's laugh boomed across the room, which sounded wrong in this swanky place with its classical music and mood lighting. But it also somehow felt exactly right. "I told you I would make it worth the drive."

"If it tastes anything like it looks, I may have to make that drive more often."

"You better try it then and tell me what you think."

She picked up her fork, hesitating. She wanted to dig in and experience this beautiful dish. She also didn't want to ruin it. The need to do more than see and smell it won out, and she plunged her fork into the butternut squash, making sure to get one of the pecans, too, and took a bite. Closing her eyes, she savored the buttery, sweet, nutty, cinnamon-y flavors exploding across her tongue. "I think this might be the best thing I've ever tasted. This is amazing, Marcus."

She cut into the crispy ball next, curious to see what it was, and found mashed potatoes with a purplish-reddish filling. With her fork holding a bite filled with the perfect amount of the inside and the outside, she brought it to her mouth and savored the bite. It was sweet and tangy and the potatoes were light and fluffy and crispy. "Oh my goodness, what is this?"

Marcus smiled. "Jackfruit, ginger cranberry sauce, mustard, maple, and a few secret ingredients."

He seemed to be genuinely pleased that she was enjoying the food he made, and she was more than genuinely pleased to be eating it. As they both ate and talked, things fell into an easier rhythm, and all the negative emotions she had been feeling over the past week and a half fled. She was glad that he had started out their meeting with the meal, because if they had to order and then wait for food, they probably would've started off by talking business, instead of this easy banter that they'd developed over the years.

She ate until she was stuffed and still would need a box to take home the extras. When she pushed her plate aside, Marcus pushed his aside as well. Then his easy-going, open expression turned nervous.

She knew the exact last time he had looked this nervous— it was right before he kissed her for the first time, on the night of the spring dance that they had both showed up to without dates. At ten o'clock on the dot that night, she had gone outside and met him by the concessions stand next to the football field. Close enough to the gym that they could hear the music coming from inside, far away enough that they weren't seen, and they had their own little dance, attended by just the two of them. After the last song that they dared stay outside for before getting back to their friends, a slow dance, neither of them had let go. Before kissing her, he had looked into her eyes with the same nervous expression he wore right now.

He scratched the back of his neck, looking down at the table. "This is hard. Especially to admit to you. I think I made a mistake. I was so excited at the thought of having an ice cream shop and Everett had pumped me up so much, the excitement made me think I could do it. But I really don't have a clue how to start a business."

She liked seeing Marcus being carefree and happy like he always was. Seeing him vulnerable and unsure of himself was so different from what she was used to seeing. It drew her to him even more.

"I realize you're probably rolling your eyes at the fact that I'm trying to do something that you've spent years learning how to do, especially when I've done none of that. And you're probably thinking how much better off the building would be in your hands. But I'm hoping that feeding you a five-star dish will make you willing to just aim me in the direction I should go. I've got lots of genuine compliments lined up and ready to go if that will sweeten the deal."

She wanted to keep her expression unreadable and stare him down for a bit. To make him sweat. It was hard to give up her chance at a business in that building after all. But she only lasted about thirty seconds—she could see the anxiety behind his eyes and besides, she lived, breathed, and slept business planning. If she was around people who could stand hearing her talk about it nonstop all day long, she probably would do just that.

"Okay," she said, pulling a fresh notebook out of her bag and opening to the first page, the spreadsheet in her brain already opened to the Creating a Business tab. The one that made her soul sing when she opened it. "Maybe we should just start out with an overview so you'll get an idea of where you need to go, then we can break them down into specifics, or if you just want the first thing broken down, we can do that."

Marcus nodded. "Sounds good. I like that plan."

"The first step is always market research." She wrote it down on the first line of the notebook. "You need to find out if the product you're going to sell is going to have a big enough customer base to warrant having a business. Obviously you don't want to open a shop selling something that is super cool if it isn't even going to bring in enough sales a month to pay the rent."

Marcus kept nodding, so she kept going.

"It'll all depend on your business plan, of course, but I think it's safe to say that there's a place for your ice cream shop in Nestled Hollow. There's nothing like it, and between locals and the number of tourists that come in a year, you'll have a good customer base. The Fire and Ice Festival was your market research on your product itself."

She put a big checkmark next to Market Research in the notebook, and she didn't miss the relief that showed on his face at having one item checked off. It was kind of cute.

Then she started talking about creating business plans and setting goals and figuring out costs. Then, of course, choosing a business structure, deciding on a business name and registering it, determining the needs for a small business loan and applying for it, then getting a business license and permit.

The more she talked about each of the items, the more excitement coursed through her. She knew all this stuff forward and backward and inside out. Many of the individual items she had participated in doing for one company she worked for or another, but it had never all been up to her. She had been dying to do all of them. All for the same company. If this were her company, she would be giddy with excitement right now. She would probably have a hard time stopping working to go to sleep each night.

Somewhere around talking about branding, pricing strategies, and coming up with an accounting system, she noticed the fear, overwhelm, and uncertainty on his face. Her hand was itching to add construction to the interior of the building, signage, look of the outside of the building, ordering the equipment, marketing, advertising, and hiring employees to the list, but she didn't think he could handle any more steps right now, so she put down her pen so she wouldn't be tempted.

Marcus ran his hands over his face, then glanced back at the kitchen doors. She didn't know if he had been away from the kitchen too long and needed to get back, or if he was looking for an escape route.

Finally he turned back and met her eyes. "I need help. More than just a night of getting aimed the right direction."

"Marcus," she said, hesitant, "I'm pretty sure Everett and Kennon would be even less okay with that than they would be with us dating."

"We don't have to partner for the business. You know that's what everyone is freaked out about. How about I just hire you as a consultant? Do you do that? I'll pay you to help me get the business up and running. There can't be any harm in that."

She put her fist on her lips, looking down at the list.

"Please? You're brilliant at this stuff, Joselyn. And I'm so lost."

"Is that one of the compliments you had at the ready in case it was needed?"

He chuckled. Not his normal happy sound—one that was colored by worry. "Remember," he said, pointing at her, "I said I'd only give 'genuine' compliments." After a few moments, he added in a low voice, "It's incredible to see how happy this stuff makes you. This business stuff makes me want to tie myself to a buoy during a hurricane, but you—you're alive with excitement."

The way he looked at her when he said that brought heat to her cheeks. Usually they just teased each other a lot—they didn't give serious compliments like he just had. They'd spent a lot of time in the same house since they broke up in high school, and had both figured out years ago exactly how much distance to give each other to keep things easygoing between them. This would break that.

But this project excited her so much. She had quit her second job nearly three weeks ago, and normally she would've started a new one long before now—one that would benefit her future business-owning-self in some way. But because she had been so sad at the loss of the business she had thought she was going to have for less than two hours, she hadn't even gone looking for a new one yet. This could be the new job that would help future her. More so than any other second job she could possibly get.

And it would prove that she wasn't sabotaging herself or backing out because of fear. A little voice said that it wasn't the same thing—it wasn't her business, so the risk wasn't the same, but she silenced that voice. If she said yes, to helping Marcus, it was a giant risk. Just a different kind of risk.

Seeing how stressed Marcus was unsettled her. It felt wrong on him. She pictured his normally big, confident, gregarious personality, welcoming everyone around and drawing them in, and she very much wanted to see that version of Marcus in an ice cream shop at the top of Main Street.

She glanced at the rest of her meal—she had eaten just over half, and it still looked beautiful on the plate, the memory of it still making her taste buds sing. Marcus might not have any business experience, but the man was skilled. Maybe it was selfish, but she really wanted her beloved hometown to have that skill right at home.

She exhaled, looking down at the notebook, then took a deep breath and met Marcus's searching expression. "This is a colossally bad idea."

"Colossally big," he said, agreeing with her while also shaking his head.

"Looks like we're in agreement, then." She reached her hand across the table and shook his. "I accept the job."

Chapter Six

*a*s Marcus plated a pepper-stuffed pork tenderloin, he thought again about how much this really very much was a colossally bad idea. It had been two weeks since Joselyn had agreed to help him, and he was blown away at the progress they had made, especially since both of them had full-time jobs with very different schedules. In trying to compensate for that, he was getting less sleep than normal, but he wasn't feeling sleep deprived. Exhausted, yes. Sleepy, no. He was being fueled by pure excitement.

Excitement, and the nearness of Joselyn. The more he worked with her, the more he experienced her passion for running a business. He had practiced for years to keep the feelings he had for her buried deep, but the more time he spent near her, the more difficult it became.

He had to keep reminding himself how important the entire Zimmerman family was to him. When people asked him questions about his family, he usually included the Zimmermans in his answer. He started counting them as family when his mom stuck him on a plane in Nestled Hollow to come live with his grandparents and he was first embraced by them. He continued when his mom and his aunt got in a deadly car wreck six months later, leaving him parentless and his grandma with two more kids living with her. He included the Zimmermans in his list of family when his grandpa died a year later. When his grandma died when he was nineteen. When he moved away to college and his cousins moved away, too.

Of course, whenever anyone asked anything even remotely about what his version of a perfect date, girlfriend, woman, or wife would be, all he could think of was Joselyn. But if he pursued a relationship with Joselyn and anything went wrong, he would lose her *and* the entire Zimmerman family. He had spent ten years keeping just enough distance between them to keep himself from falling for her any more than he already had. What had he been thinking, asking her to spend so much time with him?

Colossally bad idea, indeed.

He heard the unique buzz he had set for her texts sound from his phone on the counter behind him. Once he put the order up, he wiped his hands on a towel and went to his phone.

You close the restaurant tonight, right? Want to work on anything after?

Over the past two weeks, he had made more decisions than he normally made in a year. He had worked with Joselyn to come up with a business plan, which had more details on it than he ever would've been able to guess. They had set goals for the business. He had researched costs on his own, since he was the one with all the restaurant supply contacts, and

Joselyn had helped him to turn those numbers into pricing strategies. They had brainstormed business names quite a bit, but still hadn't come up with one. And they had started looking at other ice cream shops and brainstorming about what his should look like.

It was all exhausting, and he couldn't look at numbers or plans or strategies tonight. His brain needed a break. He needed to fill his creative well in a way that worked for him. He paused a moment, then texted, *I do. Product development.* He smiled, knowing that the phrasing probably would speak to Joselyn's business-loving soul. *How about we play around with some flavors after I get things finished here? You can be my taste-tester.*

My taste buds and I will be at the restaurant at 11:00. :)

Marcus spent the rest of his shift dreaming about ice cream flavor combinations and trying not to dream about Joselyn.

Dustin was chattier than normal tonight, and doing all the closing tasks was taking them so long. His bosses never minded him staying after to experiment with making ice cream or appetizers or entrees—they had benefitted from his new creations quite a bit over the years. But just because they were okay with him staying after to make ice cream with Joselyn didn't mean he was ready to tell them that he would be quitting yet. Not until he signed the lease papers and they could start construction on the building, and that wasn't for another five weeks.

45

But if he was being honest, that wasn't the only reason why he wanted Dustin to leave. He shouldn't want to be alone with Joselyn. Nothing could ever happen between them, so spending so much time with her was really just setting his heart up to be so much more wrecked then it had been as a teen. He knew that, and his sense of self-preservation was begging him to get distance from her constantly. But his desire to be with her always won out.

Definitely colossally bad.

The rest of the staff seemed to be in a hurry to get off work, so as soon as they left, Marcus got Dustin out the door, too. It was less than a minute after his sous chef pulled out of the parking lot before he spotted Joselyn's headlights as she pulled in. She parked at the back of the building and he held the back door open for her, trying to ignore the fact that his heart rate picked up just seeing her. She was just his business consultant.

"Good evening, Sunshine," he said as she neared.

As she walked through the doorway, the smile she gave him seemed to be filled with joy at seeing him. He drank in the smile like a man dying of thirst when he was finally given a glass of water, and instantly he knew that her expression had been burned into his memory so fully that he'd be able to pull it up again for the rest of his life.

This wasn't the first time they'd had a planning session this late at night, but it was the first time they'd had it at the restaurant, so he gave her a quick tour before getting started. Then he grabbed an armful of ingredients and started putting them on the counter near one of the cook tops, and noticed Joselyn shiver and wrap her arms around herself.

"Oh, sorry. We keep the temperature pretty cool back here because it would get too hot with all the cooking going on if we didn't. I hadn't thought it might get cold in here." He was plenty warm. He wanted to wrap his arms around her and share all his warmth with her. But that didn't exactly take him further from the colossally bad idea. He would've offered her his coat if he had thought to bring one. Why hadn't he brought one just in case?

"I'm totally fine," Joselyn said as she jumped up to sit on the counter next to him as he worked.

A thrill unlike his normal making-something-new thrill raced through him. "Will you hand me the maple syrup? It's by the sea salt 'n' honey, darlin'."

Joselyn chuckled. "Honey darlin'. Can't say I've ever been called that before." She smiled, twisting to the side and picking up the container, turning it over in her hand. "Grade B maple syrup." She took the lid off and brought it to her nose. "Oh wow—that smells divine."

"It's the good stuff. The key to making the best ice cream is to start with the best ingredients. I'm thinking of making an ice cream with a maple base, with candied bacon and toasted walnuts."

Joselyn's stomach growled audibly. "Obviously it's more than just my taste buds that like the sound of that—my stomach wants it too."

"If you're hungry, I can make you some real food."

She shook her head. "Nah. Ice cream is good."

Marcus laughed loudly. "I see you still have your ability to live off sugar alone." He cracked half a dozen eggs, separating the yolks from the whites, and putting the yolks in a sauce pan. He poured as much maple syrup as he guessed it would take into a measuring cup and then wrote down how much he was putting in. He had come up with enough new recipes to know to keep track well. He whisked the two, then turned the heat on to medium. He measured half and half and heavy cream, recording the amounts and adding them to the mix. "Remember when you and me and Kennon and Everett ran away from home?"

"I remember. You three were probably ten and I was eight."

"That sounds about right. I came over to play, but Everett said that they couldn't, because both he and Kennon were grounded until their room was clean. But Kennon said it wasn't fair for him to be grounded since it was all Everett's stuff, and Everett said he had too much stuff, so trying to tackle it all was too overwhelming."

"I believe the phrase he used," Joselyn said, "was 'cruel and unusual punishment.'"

Marcus chuckled. "I had completely forgotten that. I do remember that it was Everett who suggested that the best solution was to run away from home." He kept whisking the mix as it cooked, emulsifying the fats in the creams.

"I remember wanting in on the adventure, and you guys weren't going to let me until you realized that you'd need food if you ran away. My mom was in the kitchen making dinner, and I was the only one of us who could go get food without arousing suspicion."

"Because your room was already squeaky clean, like usual." He almost never went into her room, but he remembered walking by it plenty of times, and always marveling that another kid's room could be so pristine.

"Which was a good thing, because you three never would've survived without food."

Marcus laughed long and loud. "When we got to the spot in the mountains where we decided we were going to live, and you opened up the pack you brought of food, all it contained was four Twinkies and an unopened two pound bag of brown sugar."

"And four plastic spoons."

"I don't think you can call that 'food.'"

"I don't know—you all thought I was the most brilliant kid who ever lived when I first opened that pack."

He nodded. "Not so much after we ate it all, though. It was a good thing that you have immunity, or we wouldn't have had someone to go for help."

This time, Joselyn laughed, and the sound was like sunshine itself. He concentrated on his whisking so he wouldn't dwell on the sound of it so much. The mixture was starting to look right, so he dipped a spoon in it. When it coated the spoon, he ran his finger along the back of it. It left a clean line.

"Perfect." He removed it from the heat, strained the mix into a bowl, and then added sea salt.

As he was pouring the mix into the ice cream maker, Joselyn said, "Have you decided on other flavors yet? Or how many flavors you're going to carry? Or if you're going to have a rotating flavor, or a flavor of the month?"

"Ooo. I like the idea of a flavor of the month," he said, closing the top of the machine and heading to the sink to clean the bowl. He liked to experiment and try new things, but he couldn't do that nearly enough at this restaurant. The owners wouldn't change the menu more than twice a year, and didn't like the concept of a nightly special, or offering anything else not on the menu.

As he was placing bacon on a tray and putting it into an oven, toasting walnuts, taking the bacon out when it was almost done, draining the fat, coating it in maple syrup, then returning it to the oven to caramelize, he and Joselyn talked about flavors. Together they brainstormed, and he mentioned all the flavors he had either made or thought of making over the past few weeks. Buttered popcorn, lemonade, lavender rose, cinnamon oatmeal cookie, key lime, potato chip and pretzel, olive oil. He pulled the caramelized bacon out of the oven and set the tray on the rack to cool.

"Oh!" Joselyn said. "You should make a Dr. Pepper one. Macie would go crazy for it."

"Add it to the list."

"And maybe something specific to Nestled Hollow. Like," Joselyn looked up at the ceiling, tapping her pen on her lips, which only brought Marcus's attention to them, and he imagined how it would feel to kiss those lips for a full three seconds before he caught himself and stopped. "Nestled Hollow Heaven. Something like that."

"Good idea." Getting the thought of her lips out of his head was a little more difficult than he thought it would be. His mind scrambled for a flavor he could bring up. "I made a sea salt and honey ice cream once. It was so good I was thinking of giving up real food and only eating it."

"Wow—good enough to make a talented chef give up real food? That flavor's definitely going on the list," she said. Her pen was poised over the page in her notebook, but she hesitated, a grin spreading across her face. "You should name that flavor 'By the sea salt, honey darling.'"

Marcus laughed from deep within his belly. "Done." That flavor was going to forever remind him of Joselyn from now on. If he could only have one flavor of ice cream for the rest of his life, it would be that one, so it seemed fitting.

Now that the caramelized bacon had time to cool, he grabbed a bowl and started breaking it into it in chunks.

"Marcus. Remember how we were talking about branding? What do you think about giving all of your flavors names like that?"

"I like it." He looked down at the bacon in the bowl, the walnuts next to them, and the maple ice cream in the machine. "How about 'Maple, Please Bring Home the Bacon.'"

"Yes! Just like that!" Joselyn wrote it down in his notebook.

Marcus glanced down at his watch. The ice cream was probably at a good soft-serve hardness right now, so he took a bowl to the ice cream machine, pulled down the lever, and watched as his maple ice cream filled the bowl. He could cook all day long, but nothing excited him as much as seeing a close-to-finished batch of ice cream coming out of this machine. Once he got it all out, he carried it over to the counter where he was working and folded in the walnuts and bacon. Then he grabbed a tray and lined it with parchment paper. "This will have to freeze overnight, but I want us to try it before we leave so," he said as he spread some on the parchment paper, "I'm going to put this in the blast chiller."

A few minutes later, he used a paddle to scrape the ice cream off the parchment paper in a thin layer that rolled in on itself as he worked, then put it into a bowl. He got two spoons and handed one to Joselyn. She came over to stand right next to him, and they grinned at each other.

Joselyn's eyes sparkled with anticipation. Man, he hoped this flavor turned out.

Their spoons were headed toward the bowl when he shouted, "Wait!" He left Joselyn standing next to the ice cream, wondering why he was stopping the ice cream eating while he raced into the walk-in fridge. He found the right jar, unscrewed the lid, and pulled out a single maraschino cherry.

He headed back to Joselyn and their bowl of ice cream. "Ice cream is always better with a cherry on top. I can't believe I nearly served a bowl without one."

Joselyn gave him a questioning look, and for a moment, he

wondered if the look on her face was her thinking it was weird. Then she said, "There's your company name right there."

Now Marcus was the one wearing the confused, questioning expression. What was it he had said?

"With a cherry on top!" Joselyn said. "We could incorporate it into your logo. What do you think?"

He smiled. He loved the name. He had no idea if he loved the name because he loved the name, or if he loved the name because he loved the way the name had looked when Joselyn was saying it. "I think we can finally cross 'come up with a business name' off your list."

Joselyn's smile was brilliant and made him focus way too much on her lips again. She kept her eyes on his and moved her spoon toward the ice cream, slowly, waiting for his to match hers. So he lowered his spoon, too, and both spoons touched the ice cream at the same time. He scooped up a big enough spoonful of just the maple ice cream itself, without the bacon or walnuts, so he could really test the flavor of it.

It was every bit as creamy as he was expecting, and he moved it around on his tongue to get a good sense of the flavor. The maple zinged on his tongue, and he thought it was probably pretty close to right where it should be. He might make a note on the recipe to try a small amount less—not much less, but he didn't want it to compete too much with the taste of the bacon or walnuts.

He got a second scoop with the perfect amount of bacon and walnuts, and tested the ice cream as a whole. Man, he cooked that bacon perfectly. The maple had caramelized so well and the taste combined so well with the smokiness of the bacon and the crunch from the walnuts.

"Oh, my," Joselyn said as she finished her second bite. "When you told me the flavor we were making, I think I was imagining the maple donut bars they sometimes have at Quick Stop convenience store. I got one with bacon once. This, though. Marcus, you should be crowned king of something. King of a nation where the national food is ice cream. And the national anthem is an ode to ice cream. And the national tree is both a maple and a walnut. And the national vehicle is an ice cream truck."

"Is this market testing we've got going on right now?"

Joselyn laughed. "Yes. I can tell you that the market will love this."

Marcus's chest lightened. It would've been so embarrassing if the ice cream wouldn't have turned out well. He hoped she would like it, but her reaction made him so happy a laugh burst out of him.

Keeping his eyes on her, he scooped up another bite, and as he put it in his mouth, he noticed her gaze shift to his lips, too, and it felt like the temperature in the kitchen raised. He made his gaze go back to the bowl, and as he was getting another spoonful, he was about to ask her about something in his business plan, but then she went in for a scoop at the same time and her shoulder pressed up against his and he could no longer remember what he was going to ask. He could barely remember how to form words.

"After making an masterpiece like this," Joselyn said, picking up the maraschino cherry by the stem, "I think you deserve this." He opened his mouth as she brought it to his lips, and he held it with his teeth while she pulled the stem free.

He expected her to back away as he chewed and swallowed, but she didn't. Their faces were only a foot apart. He heard the little voices of warning trying to pull him back, but he didn't care. He'd been listening to them ever since his senior year. For the first time in years, it looked like Joselyn was feeling the same things he was. It was time to be brave.

He leaned in a little closer, and Joselyn responded by closing the gap to within two inches. Her warm, sweet breath tickled his cheek. He knew how badly he wanted this, but wanted to see how badly she did. So he waited. Her hazel eyes were warm, the build-up of weeks of working closely together, the outside ring of color a deep green, the golden tones the color of sunset.

Then she jerked away from him, the sudden loss of her nearness feeling like she had taken a part of him with her.

"I don't know what I was thinking." Her eyes were wild, looking all around the kitchen, but not at him. "That was stupid. I shouldn't have. That was bad. So bad."

Each sentence felt like a punch, taking him lower and lower. He should have listened to the voices telling him to back off—they knew what they were talking about.

"I've got to go," she said, right before grabbing her jacket and keys and racing out the back door.

He followed behind her and stood at the back door, like an idiot who forgot how to form words or ask questions. Maybe if he had said something, she wouldn't have left with terror on her face.

As he watched her get safely into her car and drive away, he realized that he hadn't forgotten how to ask questions. He was just afraid that he couldn't handle what the answers would be. It was the reason he hadn't asked them at any time in the past decade.

Chapter Seven

*J*oselyn made it nearly three blocks away from the restaurant before she had to pull over—hands shaking, heart racing—and catch her breath. She didn't know what she had been thinking. Yes, she had felt the growing attraction between her and Marcus over the past few weeks—they were working together closely and seeing each other practically every day.

But she knew what could happen if they dated. Back when they were in high school, neither of them had been shy about voicing their opinions before they started dating or during, and they didn't always agree with each other, of course. Then she read a teen magazine with a quiz in it to see if the guy you were dating had long-term relationship potential. To see if you were "soul mates." She had taken the quiz and had frozen when she got to the part that said, "How often do you disagree?" They talked about big topics every day, and even if they agreed on the big parts, there were always parts where they hadn't, so she marked "daily."

It hadn't taken a lot of time before she could look back on

the situation and see how ridiculous and wrong the quiz had been, but at the time, she hadn't had enough dating experience to know that, and they broke up over it.

She had always assumed that they would take a break for a while, and then get back together. It was *Marcus*, after all. A part of her had always known that if "soul mates" was a real thing and not just a romantic fantasy, then she and Marcus were it.

But then he left. Ran away. For a full two months, she didn't see a glimpse of him. She had lost her boyfriend and a family member when they broke up, and those two months had been the most difficult of her life. Her best friend at the time, Addison, told her that all breakups were painful and that she would be fine after a week or two. But looking back now, with a decade of dating and boyfriends and breakups in the mix, still nothing compared to that breakup with Marcus. Any thoughts she'd had of them eventually getting back together had fled when he did. She had known even back then that she would never be able to recover from a breakup with Marcus again.

So long ago, she learned how to not let feelings for him get in. Once he came back, she learned pretty quickly how to trap them behind a steel door.

Not only would it be too painful to ever date him again, he was Everett's best friend. And he was super good friends with Kennon. Her entire family accepted him as one of their own. Of all the people in the world she could date, he was the one she couldn't. Ever.

They had spent plenty of time with each other in the past ten years, and nothing had happened between them. It was the ice cream's fault. It was too good, too creamy, too sweet, too delicious, too perfect. Combine that with being inches away from the very good-smelling, very muscular, very handsome man who made the ice cream, and of course an accident happened. Or a near-accident. It was just situational.

She was just going to have to make sure she didn't end up being in that situation in the future. He didn't need her there to make the ice cream—he just wanted her opinion on tasting it.

She could do that.

If she wasn't tasting it after seeing the man so at home in a kitchen and so passionate about what he was creating, she would be fine.

Just fine.

Joselyn got stuck in a marketing strategy meeting at work, and by the time she made the hour and twenty minute drive from her work to Nestled Hollow, she was late and Marcus was already at the Elsmore Construction offices. He must have seen her pull up, because he was holding the door to the building open for her when she stepped out of her car.

He was wearing jeans and a long-sleeved blue thermal shirt that she had seen him wear a million times. Why did he look so good in it this time? He had been a broad-shoulders, big-muscles kind of guy since he was a teen, so it wasn't the way those muscles showed as his arm was outstretched toward the door, the rest of his body leaning with casual confidence. The guy smiled so much he probably smiled in his sleep, so it wasn't the way happiness at seeing her spread across his face.

It was probably because of the sun. The way it hung low and golden in the sky and reflected off the snow, bathing him in warmth. That's all it was. Ambient lighting.

He had been wary at their first meeting after she very nearly kissed him, and she probably was, too. It was hard to tell through the awkward feelings that were trying to force themselves center stage. But they were both quite well practiced at how to act around one another after they had been kissing as teens before their breakup, so being around each other after not kissing at all as adults was no big deal. It didn't matter that she was now trying to act that way when she had newfound feelings for him sneaking their way in. She could pretend with the best of them, so things had settled into a more normal state over the past three days.

Besides, she expected those feelings toward him would go away any day now. "Hi," she said as she neared Marcus, in a pretty convincing things-are-perfectly-normal voice, if she did say so herself. She was glad she had said the word when she did, because as she walked past where he stood to hold the door for her, close enough to brush against him and definitely close enough to smell the crisp cleanness of his laundry detergent, she wasn't sure she could've even said a simple two letter word correctly.

She smiled at the contractor and reached out to shake his hand. "I apologize for being late. I hope I didn't throw your schedule off. I'm Joselyn Zimmerman."

"Nate Elsmore. And not at all—Marcus and I were just chatting about Nestled Hollow High."

She knew that the contractor had grown up in Nestled Hollow and had recently moved back, and she knew that his parents owned Elsmore Market, but she hadn't remembered him. She was just glad that there was now a contractor who was based in Nestled Hollow.

"He was three years ahead of me in school," Marcus said, "but he remembers me."

"Mostly," Nate said as he motioned them to a round table with building plans on top. "I was just telling him that I was surprised to see him come through my door, because when you had called and set up the appointment for Marcus Williams, it hadn't seemed familiar. We didn't know each other too well, but I had thought his last name was Zimmerman."

Joselyn laughed right along with them. She already had twin brothers who were two years ahead of her in school. And although Marcus was beefy and dark-haired, and Everett and Kennon had more lean frames and sandy-blonde hair and the three of them were in the same grade, people still somehow always thought that they were all brothers.

Nate had already printed out building schematics on the large paper, and as the three of them sat around where it was spread on the table, he started pointing out the building dimensions, and where the front and back doors and windows were.

"I took the information that Joselyn sent me from your designer and you can see I've marked all of that in here. You've got your front counter and freezer case to display your ice cream flavors going in here, and your flow of customers will be right through here, so you'll have this space for tables and chairs. Now I've got your kitchen plans marked here—are you wanting a wall along here to separate it from the front of your store?"

"Nah," Marcus said. "I don't want to be closed off from all the action! Let's do something open."

Nate nodded, and made some notations on the plans.

"I don't want just tables and chairs, though," Marcus said. "Can we do some built-in booths along this side? Maybe a few that are smaller and more intimate and then one great big one."

"Define 'great big,'" Nate said.

"I'm talking big enough for a Zimmerman-sized family to come in. Or a little league team. Or a big group of teens after a football game. I want people to come and feel like they can be surrounded by those they love."

As Nate and Marcus continued to talk about the plans for the shop, Joselyn watched him and marveled at the passion that poured out of him when he talked about family and enjoying the company of others and bringing people together with food.

Nate tapped his finger on the back half of the building. "Since this building is much deeper than it is wide, you've got a lot of space that you'll need to decide on. You'll need a room for storage and an office for doing things like the accounting. Those will take up about this much space. So let's talk about what to do with the rest."

"I want a room right here," Marcus said, touching his thick pointer finger in the space just behind the kitchen.

Nate nodded. "Okay. The storage room? Or do you mean for the office?"

"Neither," Marcus said, shaking his head.

Nate's eyebrows drew together as he studied Marcus, trying to understand. "What kind of room?"

"Well, someday I hope to be married and have a bunch of kids." Marcus rubbed the back of his neck with his hand as he spoke, which made Joselyn wonder if he might have had doubts or fears about that. "I want them to be able to come hang out here with me and have a place to go."

Marcus had always been one of the most friendly, outgoing people she knew, but it hadn't hit her until just now how important having his own big family was to him. Even through all their deep discussions back when they were dating and their casual chats over the years since then, she never knew how much her own hopes, wishes, and desires for family matched up exactly with his.

"That sounds perfect," Nate said, almost in a whisper.

"Do you have kids?" Joselyn asked. His comment had sounded like he wished he had a room next to his office for his own.

His head jerked up from the plans, meeting Joselyn's eyes for a moment before he shook himself out of whatever he had been thinking. "Um, no. I want kids, though. I wouldn't mind having lots, either."

Joselyn glanced at the man's hand, and noticed that he didn't wear a wedding ring, yet had the indentation in his finger from having worn one for a few years. She hoped that both he and Marcus would get their wishes.

And she really wished that she could be at Marcus's side as his wife, raising with him that bunch of kids he talked about.

The unbidden thought shocked her. Did she really feel that way?

As Marcus discussed with Nate possibly turning the remaining back section into a room that could be used for birthday parties or other group gatherings, Joselyn tried to figure out when she had started to see Marcus in that way. Because even with all the admiring of the man she had been doing over the past four weeks, she had not seen that coming.

Chapter Eight

During the annual birthday breakfast at Back Porch Grill, Marcus tried to steer the conversation back to Everett and the fact that it was his birthday, but Everett and his wife Hannah still asked about With a Cherry on Top. It wasn't that he didn't like spending every waking moment talking about it, but it was Everett's birthday, not his.

"Do you know what would make a great ice cream flavor," Everett asked as he pointed his fork at his plate. "Back Porch Grill waffles with strawberry syrup."

"But then every time you got that flavor," Hannah said, "it wouldn't matter what time of the year or what time of day it was, you would think it was breakfast time on your birthday."

"I'd be okay with that," Everett said as he got another fork full of his waffles and shoved it in his mouth. His three-year-old son Drew must have decided he was finished with his waffles—or at least that he was finished licking all the whipped cream off the top—and climbed around the booth and onto Everett's lap. Everett got him situated on his lap before cutting into his next piece.

Hannah gave their one-year-old another bite of his pancake. "It sounds like you and Joselyn have gotten through a lot of the steps you need to before your shop opens."

"We have," Marcus said, pushing his plate with the part of his omelet he was too full to eat toward the middle of the table. "If I'd had to do all of this myself, I doubt I would've made it through the first month before having to close down. Joselyn is brilliant. She really knows her stuff."

Everett nodded in agreement as he took another bite.

"It sounds like the two of you have been spending a *lot* of time together over the past two months," Hannah said, not really as a statement, but as an obvious push for more information.

"Well, yeah. I mean there's a lot to do."

"Wait," Everett said before he even finished chewing his bite. "You and my sister aren't—" He scooted Drew to the seat between him and Hannah, so there was nothing between him and Marcus than the table.

"No!" Marcus said, feeling like the room suddenly got too warm. "No, of course not. She's just my business consultant." He hoped his words had been convincing. Because truthfully, nothing *had* happened between him and Joselyn. But he was too embarrassed to admit, even to himself, how often over the past eight weeks he wished something would happen between the two of them. He had very nearly kissed her a month ago, and she had made it very clear that day and in the days since that she wasn't interested in something actually happening between them. So Everett really had nothing to worry about.

But Everett wasn't taking his next bite—his fork was hovering in the air as he studied Marcus. He suddenly worried that every single motion he made was going to tip off Everett to exactly how hard he had fallen for his sister.

And then both of their phones buzzed, and they both picked them up. It was a message from Kennon to the two of them.

T minus 10 and counting!

Marcus glanced at the clock on his phone, his eyebrows drawing together. It was only 8:50. But Everett was already typing furiously, so he waited for his text to send.

Dude. I thought we were swing jumping at 10 MY TIME, not Kansas City time. We're still eating breakfast.

It didn't take long for Kennon to respond.

I'm on my way to my park as we speak.
We've been alive 30 years today, Bro.
30 years, and this is the first birthday we haven't been together to jump swings.
You're not going to jeopardize that tradition because of a time zone miscommunication, are you? Where's the love?
Marcus. I'm counting on you to get him there. Don't let me down.

Marcus grinned. His birthday wasn't for five months from exactly today, but he had been part of this tradition with Everett and Kennon since the year they turned ten. "You heard the man. We gotta go."

He called out to Dex. "Can we get some boxes and the check?"

Everett stood up so he could see over the back of the booth and held two thumbs up toward the kitchen. "Amazing birthday breakfast as always, Cole!"

"Go," Hannah said to Everett. "Ride with Marcus. I'll get the bill paid, get the kids buckled in, then come join you."

"Are you sure?" Everett said, hesitating.

Hannah glanced at her watch. "You're down to seven minutes. Go! I've got this."

Marcus raced with Everett out to his car that was parked right in front of Back Porch Grill. Since the restaurant was right at the start of Main, the park was only about a block and a half away. They probably could've run there in the amount of time they had, but this way he wouldn't leave his car taking up a restaurant parking space. He drove the short distance and hurried into a parking spot at the end of the lot closest to the playground toys, and the two of them practically leapt out of the car and raced through the snow to the swings. The day was bright and sunshiny, making it feel warm enough to melt a couple inches of snow. It was a good thing, because neither of them had thought to grab their coats.

"Four minutes," Everett said as the two of them started stretching out their calves. "Are you ready?"

Marcus nodded as he stretched his arms, too. "I've been training for this every day for the past year."

Everett froze right in the middle of stretching his quad. "For real?"

Marcus laughed loudly. "No. Not once, actually. But I do intend to beat you both—I have youth on my side, Old Man."

Everett tried to give him a playful punch in the arm, but Marcus danced out of the way.

"That's it. In five months when you turn the big three-oh, I'm going to sign your email address up for newsletters from companies that sell hearing aids, denture creams, walking canes, adult diapers, and AARP memberships."

Both their phones buzzed just then, and they both

answered the video chat from Kennon. Marcus looked toward the parking lot to see if he could see Hannah and their kids just as their car came up the hill to the park. He knew that Joselyn was at her parents' house getting ready for the big birthday bash, and he wondered for a moment if it would be weird to ask her to come. Probably so—it wasn't like they were dating. But in all the times he'd met with Everett and Kennon at this park on March 10th, this was the first time that it felt wrong not to have her here.

"Hey." Kennon's voice came through the phones, and Marcus moved next to Everett. "Okay, so I found a park in Bonner Springs that is pretty close to Snowdrift Springs Park, so it'll be almost like we are at the same park."

Marcus could see part of the park behind Kennon. "Wow —nice job! That looks about as close as you can get to the park here. You've even got some snow."

Everett glanced toward the parking lot. "Hannah is just getting Jason out of his car seat and Drew is racing toward us, so we're about ready to start. Are you ready to see how skilled we are at doing this while holding phones?"

Kennon flexed his arm, showing off his muscles. "I was born ready."

Like they had every year for the past twenty years, they took their places five feet behind the same swing they each stood behind every time and stomped down any snow that wasn't already flat. It felt strange to not have Kennon behind his swing this time.

"Go!" Kennon shouted over the phone.

Marcus took two steps toward his swing, then leaped over the seat and between the two chains holding up the sides of the seat and said "One" at the same time Everett and Kennon did. Once he landed, he turned and did the same from the other direction and said, "Two." After teasing Everett about his age, Marcus wondered how well they were all going to be able to do this when they were turning seventy and had to leap over the swings seventy times.

When they leapt over the tenth time, he and Everett both said "Ten," but he didn't hear Kennon's voice, so he glanced down at his phone, panting from the leaps they had done so far. Everett stopped too. "Bro. You're cheating on the birthday tradition? That's low."

"Not cheating," Kennon said. "I decided those swings weren't enough like the ones at home. I'm walking over to some different ones now."

Marcus noticed Hannah's face first, and whipped around to see what she was looking at that had caused that expression, Everett following his lead. Kennon, along with his wife, Rosabella and his sons, six-year-old Brian and five-year-old Brandon, were walking across the snowy field toward the swings. Kennon called out, "I decided it didn't matter how similar the park in Kansas was to this one if I didn't have you two with me."

As the three of them hugged as "birthday brothers" and said hello to Rosabella and Marcus swung Brian and Brandon in circles, he thought about how happy it made him that Kennon was able to come home for his and Everett's birthday. Almost immediately, a longing settled in right beside the happiness. He, Everett, and Kennon used to be inseparable. Then Kennon went to study engineering at the University of Kansas and stayed living there, and it was mostly he and Everett doing everything together.

The last time they had all been together was exactly a year ago. But having all three of them together, along with both of their wives and all four of their kids, didn't make Marcus feel like all the missing pieces were finally back together—it made him feel the pain his own missing piece was causing him.

He realized that he did have that feeling of everything being complete whenever he and Joselyn were in Nestled Hollow together. *That's* when everything felt right. And she was here right now, yet he hadn't seen her yet.

"Do Mom and Dad know you're here?" Everett asked.

Kennon shook his head. "What do you say we get our swing jumps in and then go surprise them?"

Marcus couldn't agree quickly enough.

This was the first time since the Fire and Ice Festival a month ago that Marcus had been at the Zimmerman family home, and he was having flashbacks to his senior year when he and Joselyn were secretly dating and he had to pretend they weren't. They weren't secretly dating now, but trying to keep his feelings hidden was difficult.

After all the excitement of Kennon's unannounced visit, then the even bigger news that Kennon and Rosabella were moving back to Nestled Hollow and were meeting with an architect to design a home in their corner of the Zimmerman plot, things went from a trip-to-the-carnival excitement level to something more resembling a trip-to-Disneyland excitement level.

When he came back upstairs from the cold storage downstairs, his arms loaded full of sparkling cider, or "celebration juice" as Momma Z liked to call it, he put all the glass bottles on the kitchen counter as he watched Joselyn across the room. She was playing some kind of clapping game with the younger nieces and nephews and they were all laughing. She wasn't just trying to keep them entertained—it was clear that she was enjoying it as much as they were, and he stopped for a moment and imagined what it might be like if it were their own kids she was playing with. It made him want to go to her even more than he already was.

Maybe it was the party atmosphere. Maybe it was spending the morning with the family he loved but wasn't the family of his own that he longed for. Maybe it was the massive amounts of time that he had spent with Joselyn over the past two months. Or the gratitude he constantly felt for her as she helped him get his business started. Or the realization that when he and Joselyn were both in Nestled Hollow, the feeling of home was more strong than anywhere he'd experienced.

Whatever it was, it made him want to walk over to her, pull her to her feet, and wrap his arms around her. He wanted to laugh with her right along with all her happy siblings. He wanted to whisper into her ear about how amazing and beautiful and brilliant she was. He wanted to tell her that she was exactly everything he wanted, needed, and ever could hope for. He wanted to kiss those smiling lips. He wanted to shout to this whole family—to the whole world—that he loved her.

But he couldn't. The longing for her to be by his side as more than a business consultant was so great he didn't know how he was ever going to be able to handle all the Zimmerman family get-togethers now that he felt the way that he did about her as strongly as he did now.

As he helped to pour the sparkling cider into clear plastic cups for this large, very varied-in-age group, Joselyn looked over at him, her face lit up with joy, and neither of them looked away. She paused, studying him, and he wanted to know so badly what was running through her mind. She cocked her head to the side ever so slightly, like she was trying to figure something out or decide something, and it felt like she could see him so clearly.

As he studied her right back, her emotions showed across her face and he felt like he could see her just as clearly. Shock must've shown across his face as he realized that she felt the same way about him that he felt about her.

Everett, Kennon, Mr. Z—the reason they were so concerned about the two of them dating was all because of what would happen to the family if they ever broke up. It wouldn't be a problem, though, if they never broke up. He had always felt that if he dated Joselyn, he would lose both her and the Zimmermans, but maybe that wasn't the case. Maybe it was possible to have both the woman he had loved for the past decade and this crazy, big, insane family.

A smile spread across Joselyn's face. A smile he knew was only meant for him, and it was the most beautiful thing he had ever seen. He hadn't ever seen that smile on her before, but he instantly knew what it was. It was a smile that felt exactly like possibility.

Chapter Nine

*J*oselyn stabbed a piece of General Tso chicken from the carton and put it in her mouth, chewing slowly as she studied her spreadsheet and her sister Macie told her about the latest failed date she had.

"I've got to hand it to you, Macie. You've got a lot of tenacity to keep searching for Mr. Right when you've found so many Mr. Wrongs lately." Joselyn clicked on another tab in her spreadsheet, this one for a dress shop she'd worked at six years ago.

"It's the only way to find that needle in a haystack. And having tenacity is better than doing nothing."

"Hey," Joselyn said. "I don't do *nothing*."

"You go on dates now and then when people ask. Name one thing you've personally done lately to find your own Mr. Right."

Like he had so much more frequently in the past several weeks, Marcus instantly came to mind. She glanced up at the clock. Eight more minutes and he would be here. She and Marcus didn't work on business plans on Sundays—they both went to their own neighborhood churches with their own group of friends. She didn't know if it was more because she had gotten so used to seeing Marcus daily or because of the understanding that had passed between them on Saturday night at her parents, but not seeing him yesterday had been almost painful.

Or at least she thought an understanding had passed between them. Once Kennon showed up at the house, things had been so crazy that she and Marcus hadn't had a chance to chat. And then it was dinner time and then cake and ice cream and then it was time for Marcus, Everett, and Kennon to take off for their annual Campfire in the Snow, and she had headed back to Denver before they returned. But he was working one of his rare day shifts today and was coming over later to do some paperwork with her. She wondered how things would go between them when she saw him again.

"The same answer as always. I'll work on finding Mr. Right when I've gotten the job side of my life figured out." Macie was the one person that Joselyn had confided to when she and Marcus had dated in high school. And if she and Marcus did start to date again, she would probably confide in Macie again. But they weren't, and her feelings toward Marcus were still so confusing that she wasn't ready to share them yet.

Joselyn clicked on another tab and half-heartedly glanced at all the info she had entered when she worked at a pet store. "I have just enjoyed helping Marcus start his business so much. For the first time, things feel like they're falling into place in my life. I find myself waking up happy before I even remember why. Every day, I'm doing what I love, but it's all just temporary. Fake. It feels like I'm accomplishing everything I've been wanting to do for years, and then I remember that it's not even for me. The building is officially Marcus's in three days, and it will officially open in a month and three days. Then that's it for me. I'm back to having dreams that I'm not putting into play."

She clicked on another tab and looked at what she had typed in four years ago after working at a toy store and sighed.

"And you're not any closer to figuring out what you want to do?"

She clicked over to the tab where she'd entered all the businesses that they had brain-stormed the day she thought she might get the hardware store for her own. "No. None of these sound as much fun as Marcus's ice cream shop. How can I go from working on something as exciting as that and then have my own business be something as boring as a laundromat?"

There was a pause before Macie spoke, and Joselyn could hear the smile in her voice. "Are you sure it's the ice cream that's exciting you and not the person you've been planning it with?"

"Macie!"

Her sister chuckled. "You don't have to answer that, as long as you're asking yourself that question."

A knock sounded on her door.

"I've got to go."

"No, wait. Just leave me on speaker phone and just set me out of the way. I'll listen to your conversation, and within five minutes, I'll be able to answer that question for you."

"*Bye*, Macie."

"You love me lots, sis. I know it."

"And you love me too."

Joselyn ended the call, set her laptop and phone on the kitchen table, and walked to her front door. She opened and her breath caught as she saw Marcus standing there, a container in his hand that she was sure held ice cream. His cheeks were red from the cold night, and his topaz eyes shone in the light outside her door. The smile on his face wasn't his normal gregarious, happy to see everyone smile—this one was more reserved, yet seemed to hold so much more meaning behind it. She could've stared at that expression for hours, trying to decipher everything behind it.

"Come in—you must be freezing! Well, not *you*, exactly, but normal people would be freezing in these temperatures."

"Punxsutawney Phil sure likes to go back on his promises. But," he held up the container, "it kept the ice cream nice and cold!"

She got out two bowls and spoons, scooped ice cream into each bowl, then took them to her little round kitchen table that barely fit in the space between her kitchen and living room. Between her notebook, her laptop, the ice cream, and the neatly stacked piles of paperwork, the table was filled.

They both sat down, and she scooped up a spoonful of ice cream as she said, "Okay, we've got a lot of legal stuff to do online and some paperwork for you to sign. We'll need to file your Articles of Organization as an LLC with the state, get your EIN number, which we'll need for you to open a business bank account, submit form one-oh-four with the Colorado Department of Revenue, the final few things for taking over the lease on Thursday, various permits, and a few random things to do with construction so that can start on Thursday too, and some to do with equipment. Then we'll need to talk about the periodic reports you'll need to file."

She was so focused on their list of tasks for the night that she'd put the bite of ice cream in her mouth without even thinking about it. Then the taste of chocolate, peanut butter, and brownies exploded on her tongue and she moaned at how incredible it tasted. "Oh my goodness. Oh, wow. I think I died and went to heaven."

She got another spoonful and put it in her mouth, closing her eyes so she could devote all her senses to tasting the creamy peanut butter, the punch of chocolatey goodness in the crisp yet chewy brownie, the silkiness of the chocolate ice cream. "I'm going to call it right now—this is my favorite flavor." She pointed down at the ice cream with her spoon as she talked, but only for a moment, because she needed it to scoop up another bite. "There's no way anything else could possibly beat this flavor. We'll just stick a blue ribbon next to its name on the menu." She put the next bite in her mouth.

"So we're calling it 'Died and went to heaven' then?"

Joselyn laughed, and then wrote exactly that in their list of ice cream names in her notebook. And then took another bite. A small part of her wanted to get right in to the exciting business stuff, but the much, much bigger part wanted to not split her attention away from this ice cream.

Unless her attention was pulled away by the man who was watching her eat his creation. Heat rose to her cheeks at his intense gaze, so she took another bite of ice cream to cool it.

"I'm glad you like it."

In much the same way that his smile was different when she had opened the door, his words came out different, too. There was so much more behind them than usual, and it made her think of all the thoughts that had been going through her mind about him in the past several weeks. She put her ice cream aside, half worried that she'd nearly kiss him again like last time, and half hoped that she could possibly ever set all her fears aside and just kiss the man.

She cleared her throat. "I think we should probably start on filing the Articles of Organization, since so many things hinge on that." She pulled her laptop to her, opened the book-mark in her browser for the Colorado Secretary of State site, and then clicked on the link they needed. Once the form was on the screen, she pushed the laptop to Marcus so he could fill it out.

Marcus started filling out the form, saying in an official sounding announcer's voice that made her laugh what he was typing into each blank as he went. He would hesitate anytime he wasn't sure on an item, and she scooted her chair closer, so they could both see the screen better—not so she could be close enough they were nearly brushing arms—and explained as they went.

About halfway through filling out the form, right after she explained the difference between an individual filing and an entity filing, Marcus pushed the laptop a few inches toward the middle of the table and turned toward her.

His gaze was intense and earnest and pleading and tender and passionate all at once. She couldn't pull her eyes away from him, even though logic was screaming at her that they were entering a danger zone. The curious side of her, though, the side that felt something strong and powerful coming from him couldn't back away. It had to know the source.

"Be my business partner."

She backed away a couple of inches, the words sounding foreign, as if her brain couldn't understand what they meant.

"Not just my consultant—be my co-owner. Run With a Cherry on Top with me."

She stood up so quickly, her chair fell backward and leaned at an angle against her couch. As she walked into her small kitchen, she ran her fingers through her hair, her back toward Marcus. After a deep breath, she turned around to face him. He still sat at the table, leaning toward her, hope and uncertainty warring on his face.

"Are you serious?"

He stood up then. "I've seen how happy creating this business has made you. I knew you always wanted your own business, but I hadn't realized how much joy it gave you until we've worked on it together the past seven weeks. I can't think of a better business partner to have than someone as passionate as you are." He stepped around the table and a couple of steps toward her. "Think of how much better this business will be if you are running it with me than if I'm running it by myself."

"But Everett—"

"Everett isn't the boss of us."

She laughed out loud, his statement somehow making her current state of shock simmer down to one of curious surprise. "As I was fond of telling him my entire childhood."

"Let me ask you this," he said. "With my ice cream and your business sense, do you think this business would fail?"

"Not a chance." The words came out immediately and with conviction.

"If we consulted each other on everything, but if you deferred to me on the product," he said, motioning to her bowl of ice cream, "and I deferred to you on business items, do you think we would have any major issues?"

She thought through it before answering, and then shook her head.

"Everett, Kennon, the entire Zimmerman clan—they're only worried if things have a high potential of not working out. And I don't think they do. Agreed?"

A smile spread across her face as she imagined how it would feel to run With a Cherry on Top alongside Marcus. Then everything wouldn't be coming to an end in five short weeks. All the tabs and tabs of potential businesses in the spreadsheet in her head could be replaced by this one business that excited her more than all the others combined. This magical feeling she had been experiencing since Marcus first asked for her help would be able to continue indefinitely. That shop at the top of Main Street would be housing her business after all.

And best of all, she would get to run it alongside Marcus. She already worried how much she would miss seeing him practically every day once she no longer had a reason to. "I think things would work out great."

"So you'll be my business partner?" He took another step toward her, his expression open and hopeful, excitement bubbling just beneath the surface.

She felt those same emotions welling up in her right alongside with a feeling of how exactly, perfectly right it all felt. "I will."

"Yes!" he shouted, and wrapped his big, muscled arms around her, picking her up off the ground and holding her close, turning around in circles in her small space.

She laughed in happiness, not sure how much was coming from herself and how much came from the happiness coming off in waves from the man holding her.

He set her gently back on the ground and instead of stepping back like a business partner should, she stayed right where she was, pressed up against Marcus, their faces a breath apart. So many times over the past several weeks when her mind wandered, she would find herself imagining moments just like this, where she was in Marcus's arms. Whenever she caught herself, she quickly directed her thoughts away from the hope of this impossibility.

But if being business partners felt so exactly right and like everything would work out, wouldn't the same be true for dating him?

As she looked into his eyes, wondering if he felt the same way, she saw a need, a longing, a yearning that matched her own. Still holding her close with one arm, he reached a hand up and placed two knuckles under her jaw, his thumb gently brushing her chin. The motion at once took her back to those blissful days as a teenager when they snuck away from everyone to bask in each other's presence. But at the same time, this felt different. Something so much stronger, forged from a decade of friendship, pulled them together now.

She rose up on her toes and pressed her lips against his. At first, his lips pressed against her so soft, so sweet, a feeling of respect and devotion coursing through her, and she felt cherished in a way she hadn't experienced before. A warmth burned in her chest at the realization of how much she had cared for this man over so many years without her being willing to recognize or admit it. The way his lips carefully, gently pressed against hers, the more she felt that the same might be true for him.

The power of that realization burned so strongly that she moved her hands from his chest to his shoulders, her fingers resting on those strong muscles, and he responded by moving his hand from her jaw to the back of her neck, tangling his fingers into her hair. The heat of the kiss burned into her as he slanted his lips against hers, and her hands moved to the back of his neck and into his hair, holding him close, not wanting to ever let go.

When they finally parted, she looked up at him, dazed and breathing quickly, drinking in that strong jaw, that open, friendly face, those welcoming eyes. He was looking at her in a way that she wanted to bottle and keep forever.

Marcus chuckled as he reached out and brushed two fingertips along her temple. "Most people shake hands when they become business partners, but I'll take this any day."

Joselyn laughed and placed one more quick kiss on his lips, as if it was sealing the deal.

Chapter Ten

*M*arcus smiled at Joselyn as they came to a stop at the end of the freeway off ramp leading into Nestled Hollow, and she gave him a brilliant smile back. Today was his day off, and Joselyn had managed to take the afternoon off. The building was officially theirs as of a couple of hours ago, and they were meeting Nate Elsmore at the shop to talk about the construction before heading back to Denver to meet their designer. After Joselyn agreed to be his business partner and they got everything submitted Monday night, he had given his work notice that he would be leaving at the end of the month.

In the two and a half days since he and Joselyn had kissed, they had made time to get together to work on the business even though he had worked both Tuesday night and Wednesday night, only a sliver of time between eleven and midnight. And most of that time had actually been spent kissing instead of working.

He pulled into a parking spot right in front of the building and he and Joselyn didn't get out of his car right away—they just looked at the building. All of the Larry's Hardware signs had been removed and the window displays were empty for the first time Marcus had ever seen. Normally, a building like this would've given off an abandoned feel to him, but right, sitting next to his business partner and the woman he had been in love with for as long as he could remember, all he could see were possibilities.

"Let's go check out our building," he said, feeling like he was twelve again and he was standing at the gates of Water World with his two cousins and his grandma and grandpa, about to go inside and experience the magic he'd spent months anticipating.

He wanted to grab hold of Joselyn's hand as they stepped over the melting mounds of snow that probably wouldn't fully melt for another few weeks, but they hadn't shared news of their relationship to the Zimmermans, and they couldn't be seen in town holding hands until they did. So he just opened the front door for her and let her walk in first and he followed closely behind.

The building was strangely different without all the shelving that Larry had used in his store. Nate and his crew were already inside, working to tear up the old laminate flooring that had seen decades of use. Everything was bare to the walls. Every scrape of the tools as they went under the flooring, the *reeeek* and then crack each chunk of laminate made as it was removed, every footstep and each word exchanged, all bounced around in the empty space, echoing and making the space feel even larger.

"Good afternoon!" Nate got up from where he was working with his crew on the flooring and, with a smile spread across his face, made his way across the remnants of broken laminate to where they stood. He motioned around the room. "It doesn't look like much yet—"

"It looks like everything," Joselyn breathed.

Marcus nodded. "It's perfect. And ours."

"Ours?" Nate asked.

"Joselyn and I are now co-owners of With a Cherry on Top."

"Congrats to you both, then!" Nate reached into his pocket and pulled out a set of keys. "Larry met me early this morning to give me the keys and asked me to present them to you."

He held them out, midway between Joselyn and Marcus, dangling from their ring. Marcus gave Joselyn a nod, and she held out her hand, palm up. He held his right under hers, and as Nate dropped the keys into her hand and she closed her fingers around them, he wrapped his fingers around her hand. She looked at him, then, with a smile so filled with excitement that he wanted to cup a hand behind her head and bend down to touch his lips against that smile. Instead, he just returned an equally excitement-filled smile.

"Let me show you around the place," Nate said. He walked them through the building, motioning to where the built-in booths would be, the front counter, the back counter, and the edges of each room, walking them along what would eventually be the hallway leading back to them.

"The storage room Larry used in the back is almost exactly what we had planned for your party room. Which means that this room that he used as an office," Nate said as they made their way back to the only structure that kept the room from being one giant rectangle of emptiness, "is very nearly the same dimensions of what we were planning for your 'extra' room."

He led them inside the room then unhooked the tape

measurer from his belt and pulled out the metal tape over and over until it had spread from the outside wall to the door. "This direction is six inches wider than we had planned, which would take six inches from the hallway. And this direction," he said as he measured from one inside wall to the other is about a foot less than we had planned. Now we can certainly tear out these two walls and get the dimensions exactly as we had planned, or we can use the room as is and save you some construction costs. I'll give you both a minute—walk around the room, discuss it, see what you think."

Marcus walked around the space, imagining the finished room he wanted built for his someday kids to play in. As easily if it was already there, he could imagine the room with a play area, a bookshelf next to a big fluffy rug and squishy seats for reading pen, toys, books, and little kids enjoying it all. He could also just as easily picture Joselyn being the mother of those children. He could picture the two of them taking turns playing with the kids and working the counter, and stealing moments when no one was in the shop to be back here as a family.

He glanced at Joselyn and wondered if she was picturing the same thing that he was. Since they were alone, she turned and stepped right up to him, just inches separating them, her face turned upward toward his. "I think it's perfect just as it is."

A golden light shone in the window from the afternoon sun as if it was there just to showcase the way Joselyn's jaw line curved from her beautiful ear to where it curved into her chin. He reached up and ran a fingertip along the line. "I think *you're* perfect." Her silky brown hair hung in big waves just past her shoulders and looked bronze in the sunlight.

She grinned and grabbed his shirt with both hands and pulled him toward her, then planted a kiss on his lips.

He smiled into her kiss and raised an eyebrow. "Kissing me in Nestled Hollow, right next to a window without blinds. Daring."

She laughed and gave him one more quick kiss. "We're about to start our own business. *Us*. Me and you together. I think it's safe to say that we've made it a habit of walking on the wild side."

⌇

It would've been difficult to leave their new building and seeing the progress Nate and his crew were already making if it had been for any other reason than to go shopping for items with their designer.

They grabbed sandwiches from Joey's Pizza and Subs, ate them in the car on the way back to Denver, and barely made it to where they were supposed to meet the designer in time.

Since they were no longer in Nestled Hollow, Marcus reached out for Joselyn's hand as they walked in and she slipped her hand into his. He relished the feeling. No matter how many years passed or how old they got, he couldn't imagine the feeling of her soft skin against his ever becoming something that didn't take his breath away.

As soon as they stepped inside the building, Marcus felt overwhelmed. It was like big-box home improvement store had married an interior design studio, and they decided to cater to businesses instead of homes. He trusted Joselyn when she said they needed to hire a designer, and he had never agreed more fully than he did at that moment.

"Marcus, Joselyn," Sandra said in her slight Texan accent as she walked over to them, her stride purposeful, her heels clacking on the floor. The woman's auburn hair was pulled back into a twist, showing off her dangly earrings. Even in those high heels, she was still shorter than Joselyn. She grabbed Marcus's free hand in one of hers and Joselyn's with her other hand, so the three of them made a circle of hand-holding. "When I first started working with the two of you, you were just business owner and consultant. And look at you now! Business partners and, judging by your hands and the looks on your faces, you've become even more than that."

Marcus opened his mouth to reply, but the woman had already dropped their hands, turned around, and motioned for them to follow as she strode away. "Now come along— we've got lots to do!"

She led them into one of a few smaller rooms that were set up like offices for designers to use and she sat them down at a table, a design portfolio resting on it. "Last we talked, it was before you became business partners. Do you still want the overall look to be welcoming, fun, open, and not cluttered?"

They both nodded, so as Sandra turned the portfolio so it was aimed toward them, she said, "Okay, I've got a couple different designs for you." She pulled out a regular-sized piece of paper from the portfolio and placed it to the side. "I've kept the same color scheme as your logo, of course, but I've lightened the colors a bit. We don't want things to be quite so 'in your face' for your customers as it would be if we kept them this bright and bold."

She flipped open the portfolio to a design on a large piece of paper, looking at the inside of the building from the perspective of the front door. Light gray tiles covered the bottom half of the walls and cyan paint filled the space above. Pink lights lit columns on either side of the left wall between the front and back counter. The With a Cherry on Top logo was big on the wall, centered between the two columns of light. The pink lights also shone down from under the countertop onto the bottom half of the front counter.

He reached out a hand to touch the design. "Wow, Sandra! This is incredible." His eyes lingered on it for a few more moments before he looked over at Joselyn to see her reaction. He couldn't tell what she thought of it by her expression, so he raised an eyebrow in question.

"It's nice. I like it."

His eyebrows drew down as he looked back at it. He thought it was way more than 'nice.'

"For a different take, I've also designed this," Sandra said, moving the first paper out of the way, revealing a second image of the store from the same perspective, but designed differently. This one had giant circles painted on the wall at the right, each one a good foot in diameter. Several were piled up on side, moving to fewer on the other, like they were spilled out of a giant bucket. They were in four different colors, all of which went well with the logo. Several other of the large circles were painted here and there on the other walls, but not nearly as many as that biggest wall. It kind of made the whole place look chaotic. Compared to the first design, this one was awful. Maybe if he hadn't seen the other design first, he would —nope, he decided. He still wouldn't like it.

"Oh, I love this," Joselyn breathed.

Marcus's attention flew to her. "Really?"

"You don't?"

He shook his head. If it was about something else, he would've probably just gone with what Joselyn said. But he was going to have to look at this every single day, and he just couldn't.

"Ooo!" Sandra said, clapping her hands like this was an exciting show she was watching. "This is the first time you two have disagreed about designs. Interesting. Okay, Marcus, tell me what you like about the first design."

Marcus reached out and pulled the first design closer. "It looks fun. There's lots of interesting things going on, and it has nice clean lines."

Sandra nodded, then said, "Joselyn—tell me what you like about the second."

"All the color. And..." she moved her hands around, like she was trying to capture some feeling in a word, "the movement, I guess."

Marcus ran his hands over his face. He and Joselyn had agreed on so many things that it hadn't occurred to him that they might find things they disagreed on. At least not when it came to the design. They had agreed to always defer to the other person when it was their area of specialty—the ice cream for him, and business decisions for her—but they hadn't taken design into consideration when they'd made that rule.

Sandra studied both of them for a moment before giving a single sharp nod and pushing both designs to the other side of the table, revealing the same image of the inside, but one that was void of any design elements. Then she got out a pencil and a package of colored pencils and went to work. Marcus was surprised she wasn't using a laptop to make a new design so she could color an entire wall with a click of a mouse, but with as quickly as her hands moved, maybe she had found that a laptop slowed her down.

"These will be thick slats of wood starting on the ceiling right above the half wall at the back counter, out just past the end of the front counter," she said as she finished drawing the last lines, "so it will look almost like an awning over the ordering area. And we'll paint them the four colors from the second design. That way we'll bring in more color and have the clean lines that Marcus likes."

Then she started drawing lines down the walls, and making them look three-dimensional. "We'll do some build-outs a few feet wide and an inch or two away from the wall to break up this big long wall into smaller sections. Then we can paint them different colors." She drew some diagonal lines on a few of the sections of wall that were recessed. "Then we'll have some one-inch trim spaced a few inches apart repeating at an angle on some of these, bringing in the movement that Joselyn likes."

"We'll do the same on this wall for uniformity and to carry the theme throughout. In these two recessed sections," she drew a giant ice cream cone with a single scoop of ice cream on top, "we can have your builder cut out a shape of an ice cream cone and I will paint it like your signature flavor."

Marcus watched in amazement as the whole thing came together, like she was putting together a puzzle. As she added in the last of the color, it was as though had just placed the last piece and everything felt right.

She turned the design their direction. "What do you think?"

"It's perfect," Joselyn said, and then looked over at him, her expression a mix of apprehension and excitement.

Marcus let out a breath of relief. "I think so, too." The whole time Sandra had been drawing the new design, he just kept thinking back to the reason why Joselyn had broken up with him back in high school—because of disagreements—and he worried that they were heading down the same track again. Luckily, Sandra was good at what she did and got them past that.

Or at least he thought they were past it. Sandra took them out onto the floor of the building so they could do some shopping, and stopped to look at tables first.

"We've got two great options on tables. They're both the same width—we've got that one that's square with rounded corners, and then that one that's a circle."

"Circle," Marcus said at the same time Joselyn said, "Square."

"Why circle?" Joselyn asked him, baffled. "They are the same width, but look how much more space the square one has! Then everyone isn't having to crowd each other, and you don't get your drink cups mixed up with someone else's."

"Because if you're in there with four of your friends or family, enjoying an ice cream cone, you each take one side of the table. If other people come in who are also your friends or family, you can't just say, 'Come on over and join us!' because there's not enough space to put two people on one side of a table this size, and it's awkward to have someone sit at the corner. With a round one, you can just keep adding more chairs. How much space do you really need when you're eating ice cream, anyway?"

Sandra rubbed her hands together in excitement. "This is so much fun! I never would've guessed there would be this many disagreements between you two. Maybe it's because you started dating. You know what they say—'opposites attract.' Okay." With her hands still clapped together, she swayed them from the left to the right, like a pendulum swinging from one of them to the other. "I'm going to say that this round goes to..." she held out the word, and then aimed her hands toward Marcus, "the gentleman wanting the round tables. With all the straight lines we're putting in the room, the round tables will contrast nicely."

Marcus put his arm around Joselyn's shoulders and kissed her temple to hopefully soften Sandra's declaration.

He wished that was the last time they disagreed. But they had very different opinions about chairs, paint colors, lighting, uniforms for employees, and signage. Each time, Sandra would declare one of them a winner of that round and explain her reasons why, each disagreement seeming to bring the woman even more joy. He wished he could've felt joy about it. Instead, even though each of them had "won" about the same number of rounds, the fact that they were disagreeing so much filled him full of worry.

Exhaustion settled in as he drove Joselyn back to her apartment once they finally finished. Between the excitement of seeing their building for the first time and the mental toll of making so many decisions with the designer and the emotional toll of the worry about how their disagreements might affect their relationship, Marcus was ready to crash.

But when he walked Joselyn to her front door, she turned and smiled at him in a way that made every negative emotion and all the exhaustion in his body whoosh out of him. She placed a hand on either side of his face, down low where two fingers were on his neck and two were on his jaw, and he closed his eyes for a moment to let the warmth of her touch wash over him.

"We made so many huge strides forward today."

He smiled and settled his hands on her hips. "That explains why today felt like it was a week long."

She laughed, a musical sound that his ears seemed to be tuned perfectly for. "You work until late tomorrow, right?"

"Until midnight. But I'll be there with you with bells on to help Macie move into her apartment the next morning."

Her fingers slid from the side of his neck to the back, her fingers running through the hair at the back of his neck, sending shivers down his spine. Then she pulled him forward and pressed her lips against his—a kiss that told him that nothing could possibly be wrong between them.

Chapter Eleven

*B*right and early on Saturday morning, Joselyn was already at Macie's brand new apartment when Marcus, her parents, and four of her siblings showed up to help Macie move in. They all made it to the door at the same time, but Marcus was the first to walk in.

"Good morning, Sunshine!" He glanced around at the empty apartment. "Macie! Nice digs you've got here. I love what you've done with the place."

"Thank you," Macie said. "I'm thinking of turning pro."

Marcus's booming laugh echoed through the empty apartment, and Joselyn realized how much she had always loved that easy, quick laugh that always rumbled throughout whatever space he was in. And not in the way that she loved Everett's laugh. How had she not noticed the difference between how they made her feel all these years? It seemed so obvious now.

Before they actually carried any boxes or furniture inside, though, her family scattered through the empty apartment to check out every room, look in every closet, and open every cupboard and drawer. It was practically Zimmerman family tradition.

The apartment was narrow and two stories high—a living room, the kitchen, and a bathroom were on the main floor, and two bedrooms and another bathroom were up a long flight of stairs. It was just old enough to really have character. Joselyn headed upstairs first to check out what would be her future room, and Macie's dogs Reese and Lola bounded up after her. After Marcus had left her apartment on Monday night—when they had decided to be business partners and shared their first kiss—Joselyn had called her sister, hoping that her offer to share an apartment was still on the table.

Macie had actually squealed when she told her the news and asked about the apartment. Macie hadn't squealed since she was about sixteen—back when they shared a bedroom instead of an apartment. Joselyn's still had her apartment in Denver until the end of the month, so she wouldn't be moving in until next weekend. First she needed to share the news with her family.

Joselyn was checking out the kitchen and Marcus was upstairs with Everett when Everett called downstairs to Macie, "Hey, Sis. You've got two bedrooms up here—you going to get a roommate?"

Macie glanced Joselyn's direction from where she stood in the living room, and Joselyn gave her a nod. So Macie called up the stairs, "Yep! Joselyn."

From all directions of the house, her family seemed to emerge at the same time, being pulled toward that declaration whether they wanted to or not, heads cocked in confusion and curiosity. Joselyn shook her head, chuckling.

"You're moving back to Nestled Hollow?" Nicole asked. "When?"

Joselyn nodded, not being able to stop the smile that spread across her face. "Next Saturday."

"That's going to be quite the commute to work," her mom said. "What made you decide that?"

Joselyn made eye contact with Marcus as everyone took the last few steps to congregate in the empty living room. Marcus gave her a smile that made her want to sigh in happiness, but she worked hard not to let it show. She waited for him to come stand next to her, and then she said, "Actually, I put my two-week's notice at work, so it will only be a week of commuting." Joselyn looked at Marcus, their grins a mirror of each other's. "Marcus and I have decided to be business partners and run With a Cherry on Top together."

The emotions crossing her family's faces ranged from elation on her mom and Macie, to interest on Nicole and Oliver, to wariness and concern on her dad and Oliver, to hurt on Everett.

"We know you might be worried about this arrangement," Marcus said, "but trust me: you should be more worried about us *not* teaming up. You've all tried my ice cream and know it's good, right?"

They all nodded, and Everett said, through emotions he was obviously trying to control, "It's the real deal."

"Well, making it and welcoming customers is all I'm good at. Beyond that, I don't know the first thing about running a business." He nodded at her parents. "Your daughter," then he nodded at the others, "your sister, is brilliant. She has poured so much into this business that she deserves to be at the helm, leading it past opening day."

Joselyn smiled and looked down, not willing to let her family know how much his words affected her.

"Then you have our support," her dad said, leaning

forward to shake Marcus's hand. "One hundred percent." He shook her hand, too, and then everyone was coming forward to congratulate them.

Her dad—and all of them—would do just what he said, support them one hundred percent. That's what Zimmermans did for each other. But that didn't make their reservations go away. She could still see the worry on their faces. She wanted to reach out and grab Marcus's hand and tell them all that they were now dating, too, but she worried that telling them about that and the business would be too much to process, and the business was the most time-sensitive.

So, instead, she said, "What are we all standing around for? We have a trailer to unpack!"

A few trips out to the trailer later, Joselyn carried a box labeled "Bedroom" into Macie's room, and found her sitting on the floor, putting two sides of a metal bedframe together.

"Help me?" Macie begged. "They're about to bring up my box spring and mattress, and I'd rather they put it right where it goes."

"Sure." Joselyn set the box against the wall and sat down at the other end of the metal frame and started sliding two pieces together.

Macie glanced at the doorway. "I see you chickened out on telling everyone that you and Marcus are dating."

Joselyn shrugged. "Baby steps."

"How is everything going with you two?"

Joselyn glanced toward the door, too, even though she knew that the stairs were creaky enough that they'd have no trouble knowing when someone was coming. She thought of the way Marcus looked at her, especially when they saw each other for the first time that day. And the way he kissed her and wrapped his arms around her and laughed his big, booming laugh at all her jokes, and listened to all her stories, and looked at her in awe when she started talking business.

She knew that between her blush at the thoughts and whatever expression she wore on her face that she had given pretty much everything away, especially when Macie laughed softly. "I take it things are going well."

"They really are." She slid the latch into place so the side she was working on wouldn't close up and moved to the corner. "Except," she said, pausing with one rail in each hand, "we've kind of been disagreeing a lot."

Macie raised an eyebrow in question, waiting for her to continue.

"Things were going really great when I was just his consultant. As soon as we started dating, though, we started having very different opinions on everything. They're not end-of-the-world things, of course, but I don't know. It still kind of worries me."

"That sounds normal," Macie said as she used her fist as a hammer to coax the two sides together.

"It does?"

"Well, yeah. Before, all of the decisions were up to only Marcus. I'm sure there were plenty of decisions to be made before you decided to be partners, right? Did you agree with every single choice he made?"

Joselyn thought for a moment. "No."

"Now, though, you're business partners. You didn't have a vested interest in the details before, but you do now. Two people are making the decisions, not just one. You're not going to agree on everything, because no two people do. That's just not the way it works, as a business partnership or as a couple in a relationship."

"True." It did make sense. Perfect sense. Logical sense. Add to her spreadsheet sense.

But that didn't stop the nagging feeling inside that it wasn't just because they were business partners or because they were a couple in a relationship. She worried it was because they were both. And the last time that they broke up over disagreements, before they even got a chance to work it out, Marcus had disappeared for two months.

"And it's the fear talking," Macie said right as Everett and Marcus started up the stairs with the box springs.

"What?" Joselyn protested. She was just shoving the last two pieces together and pinched the thin skin between her thumb and forefinger. She yelped and pulled her hand back, immediately putting the hurt hand to her mouth.

"The fear of having your own business."

Joselyn wanted to tell her sister how wrong she was. She was the older sister of the two of them, after all—if either of them should be teasing the other of being afraid, it should be her teasing Macie. But Marcus and Everett walked in the room right then, and if she was afraid—which she wasn't—she didn't want either of them to think she was.

After making more trips out to the trailer and bringing several boxes into the kitchen, she was making her way back out as Oliver brought in a box. "I think there's only one more box out there."

"I'll get it." She walked out and stepped into the enclosed trailer, and then headed toward the box at the darker end.

Marcus bounded into the trailer just then and wrapped his arms around her, turning her a complete circle before planting a kiss on her lips. From where they stood when they came to a stop, he was facing the opening at the end of the trailer, so some light made it to his face—just enough to see the ever-present smile on his face that she now recognized was slightly different for her than it was for anyone else. No matter how tired she was, that smile always gave her a boost.

"That was a long time to be in the same rooms as you without being able to wrap you in a hug."

"I know; I'm sorry. I would've told them about us, but—"

"I get it. I saw their faces. I think it was a good idea to let them get used to the business before we bombard them with anything more. As long as I can still sneak in a kiss here and there, it's all good."

"Really?"

He nodded. "And a date."

She cocked her head to the side. "A business-planning date?"

"Nope—a real date. Tonight. Like the kind that couples go on who aren't four short weeks from opening their first business. What do you say?"

"I say," she said as she wrapped her arms around his neck, "that you are definitely the one with brilliant ideas."

Then she kissed that smile that he always saved for her alone.

Chapter Twelve

*M*arcus had his eyes closed, soaking in the feel of Joselyn's lips against his, her body pulled close to his, the smell of peaches and cream shampoo that he had forever associated with her. The two of them were lost in a bubble where only they existed.

At the sound of a creak from the end of the trailer, his eyes flew open. Joselyn's dad had just rounded the corner, probably to check to see if they had gotten all the boxes, and met eyes with him. Marcus froze, but just like he'd expect from Mr. Z, the man quietly ducked away. Joselyn pulled back and turned around to see what had spooked him, but she didn't see anyone, and must've thought his reaction was just fear of getting caught.

"We should probably head back in," she said, then gave him one more quick kiss. He picked up the final box and as they walked toward the open end of the trailer, she said, "I assume tonight will be in Denver?"

His head was suddenly so full of worries that he just looked at her, not understanding what she was talking about.

"Our date. Since we haven't told my family..."

"Right. Denver."

They stepped out in the sunlight, and Joselyn glanced around, like she was seeing their surroundings for the first time. "How long were we in there? It felt like time stopped, but now I'm wondering if we were gone long enough that everyone's wondering where we went."

He suddenly wished he wasn't holding a box so he could run his hands through his hair or over his face just so he could feel like he was doing something to make sure it wasn't obvious he had just been kissing Joselyn.

Not that it mattered at this point. Mr. Z had seen, and it felt like high school all over again. Back then, the situation hadn't been much different than it was today. He and Joselyn had been secretly dating and the only person who knew was Macie. He had brought Joselyn home one night, and instead of parking in the driveway and walking her to the front door like he would have done if her family had known they were dating, he parked in front of the house Oliver and Audra were building. Parking there wasn't unusual, considering how many Zimmermans now had driver's licenses and old, beat-up cars. Then he walked her to the side of the garage. They had pretended that the space between two large shrubs was her front porch, and he gave her a goodnight kiss.

The kiss hadn't been overly long, but they had been talking and making plans for their next date with his arms around her waist and their faces inches apart. Right as they both went in for the kiss, Joselyn's dad walked around the corner of the garage, probably to get the garbage cans to put out at the curb. Marcus heard his footstep on the gravel and his eyes had flown open just as Mr. Z had noticed them in the faint moonlight.

And just like this time, their eyes had locked before Mr. Z ducked away, and Joselyn never knew.

Both times, Marcus knew, though, that he was somehow letting down the Zimmerman family.

They went back into the house and got the last of the larger items in place and helped unpack. The whole time, he could feel Everett's inner conflict about he and Joselyn becoming business partners—the desire to be supportive of his best friend, and his worry and irritation that he and Joselyn made that decision when they knew he was against it. He knew he wouldn't hear anything about it from Everett today. Everett had never been one to discuss something when he was angry. But he would bring it up soon enough.

Marcus shook his head. What would Everett say if he also knew that Marcus was dating his sister?

Mr. Z didn't come talk to him, either. Marcus knew he wouldn't—it was one of the things he respected most about Joselyn's dad. Marcus knew that Mr. Z saw him and Joselyn kissing. Mr. Z would expect that knowledge alone would make Marcus hesitate long enough to ask himself if it was right. And it *was* enough to make him hesitate—ten years ago and now.

In fact, he suddenly wondered if he had possibly sabotaged their relationship all those years ago without realizing it, just so he wouldn't be sabotaging his relationship with the entire Zimmerman family.

All he knew was, for a kid who had dealt with a lot of loss, that two months away had been the most difficult of his life.

"Where are we going?" Joselyn asked as she buckled her seat belt.

Marcus glanced over his shoulder as he backed his car out. "Well, there's still too much melting snow to go up in the mountains for a picnic like we used to, so I figured we'd do another kind of throwback date, especially since we need to end up in Denver anyway."

Joselyn's face lit up. "We're going to Champion Fun Center?"

It had definitely been the right choice. While doing so much business planning over the past two months, they had spent plenty of times alone in quiet places together. The fun center was the opposite of that in every way possible, and gave their bodies some good exercise instead of just their minds.

After a game of bowling that Joselyn won, eighteen holes of miniature golf that he won, eating snow cones that made their tongues blue, and playing their fifth round—the tiebreaker—at the basketball arcade machine, Joselyn jumped up and down at her win. He gave her a double high-five, and she immediately wound her fingers in his. They brought their entwined hands to their sides, and Joselyn gave him a kiss that turned into a smile almost as quickly as she touched her lips to his.

"You know what this win means."

"Joselyn. Come on. Let's be reasonable about this."

"You agreed to the rules before we started." She let go of one of his hands and pulled him toward the snack bar with the other.

"The cheese they put on those nachos isn't even real food! I can make you some queso dip. Really good queso dip."

"Nope. We're getting the nacho sauce of our youth."

"I made my queso for my cousin Beth, and she said that it was so good that it is now in the top spot on her 'If I could only have one food for the rest of my life' list."

Joselyn stopped, put a hand on her hip, and raised an eyebrow in challenge. He took the moment not to hold out, like he was undecided and needed her to convince him, but just to really look at her. At how beautiful she was with her face flushed from the speed basketball, hairs that had fallen out of her ponytail framing her face. He had seen a million different looks on her over the years from sleep-deprived to formal to sick in bed to business to working in the yard and everything in between, and she was breathtaking in all of them. Probably because there was so much goodness inside her that it couldn't help but spill out.

"Okay," he finally relented and let her pull him to the snack bar. He'd known he would do anything she asked from the start, but still.

As he sat across from Joselyn at a small round table, smiling and laughing and eating fake cheese that he couldn't believe he ever thought was "liquid gold sent straight from above," he realized this was why he thought it was okay for them to date and to be business partners. Because when he was with Joselyn, everything felt right in the world.

When he considered her whole family in the equation—the family he had long ago claimed as his own and didn't think he could ever live without—the waters got so much murkier. Murky enough that it had stopped him from enjoying *this* for a full decade. Murky enough that it made him question this thing that was so obviously right.

Chapter Thirteen

*M*aybe it had been a mistake for her to move in with Macie and Marcus to move in with Everett last Saturday. Neither of their leases was up until this Saturday, but they had figured it would be less stressful to get out early and have time to fully clean their old apartments if they could do it in spare time over the week, instead of rushing to do it on moving day. And they figured it might be easier to be in Nestled Hollow with all the business stuff they needed to do.

They had been wrong. They had both been living in town for a total of five days, and between the nearly two-and-a-half hours it added to their daily commutes—both of them with completely different schedules—cleaning their old apartments, unpacking the new ones, and so many business details to attend to, they were both tired, overworked, and irritable. All the fun they'd been having getting the business together for nearly ten weeks was now gone. The grand opening was in sixteen days, and they weren't even close to being ready.

Marcus had the day off, so he had spent it at the shop,

helping Nate and Sandra with getting many of the things in the shop itself ready. Joselyn had taken off work early so that she could spend an hour in the shop before they headed to their very first Main Street Business Alliance meeting, but the Colorado Avalanche were playing at the Pepsi Center tonight and traffic was already a nightmare.

By the time she got on I-70 and had relaxed a bit, she got a call from Marcus. She had answered it through her phone's speakers, so she got to hear nice and loudly that there was a minor mishap at the shop and to make sure she stopped by before the meeting.

She pulled into an empty spot in front of With a Cherry on Top more than two hours after she had left work—a trip that normally took her seventy minutes—and forced herself to take a few slow breaths. The outside of the building looked great. Whatever was wrong on the inside they could deal with. Tomorrow was her last day at work, so they would have plenty of time to deal with things.

She walked inside the building, and her attention was drawn for a small moment to the back counter, which looked less done than it had last time she had been in here. Her eyes only landed there a moment before they were drawn to Marcus, Nate, and Sandra, who seemed to be closing ranks, all with faces full of trepidation.

"What is it?"

Sounds of construction come from the kitchen—hammering and sawing and so much more noise than usual, from fans, maybe. And possibly a generator. Over the top of the half-wall, she could see a handful of heads turn toward her with their own worried looks that only made the churning stomach and tightening chest worsen.

Marcus broke free from the others and walked toward her,

arms outstretched like he was going to wrap her in a hug, but she didn't want to be protected from this. She wanted the whole truth. Now. So she held up a hand. "Tell me."

"The ice cream machine was delivered today. A full week early, even." He tried to give an enthusiastic smile, but then his shoulders fell, and he shifted to motion toward the kitchen. "It actually wasn't helpful to have it early, because the flooring isn't down yet back there. One of the delivery men stumbled and fell into the machine just a few feet from getting it into place. You've seen how big they are. Anyway, it kind of tipped, hard, since it had his weight adding to it, and, well..."

Marcus trailed off, so Nate finished. "It fell into the wall and broke it. That wouldn't have been too bad, except that part of the wall had the sink on this side of it, and so it broke water pipes."

Joselyn's hands flew to her mouth as she stepped around them to where she could see behind the front counter. The remnants of water flooding the floor were visible now, and she could see where the wall was crashed in. The sink had fallen over, and had taken that entire section of cabinets with it.

"*This* was your 'minor mishap'?"

"Now don't you worry about the cabinets or the sink," Sandra said as she clacked over in her heels to stand beside Joselyn, but just enough behind her to put a hand on each of Joselyn's shoulders, like she wanted to direct where she looked. "Those things can be replaced no problem."

The way she said it made Joselyn realize there were things that couldn't be replaced so easily. "And the ice cream machine? Is it fine?"

"It might've been if it hadn't fallen where it did, and if the delivery man hadn't been quite so hefty. They had to take it back, but they think there's a chance they'll be able to get a new one here before opening day."

"We need it *before* opening day, because we'll have to have all the ice cream ready to go."

"We'll figure something out," Marcus said.

"We will," Sandra said. "We'll figure out that and the problem with the flooding and the electrical."

Confusion hit Joselyn for a fraction of a second before panic did, and she ran toward the opening in the hallway that led into the kitchen. The flooding was so much more significant in the kitchen area. Pipes were broken and exposed and the sub-flooring and the bottom several inches of the sheetrock were both soaked. Giant, industrial-sized fans were blowing through the area, trying to dry everything out. The cords to the fans, though, weren't going to the wall outlets; they were headed out the back door, to where she was now sure that she was hearing sounds of a generator.

And that's when Sandra's comment about the electrical wiring sank in. "And the electrical?" she croaked.

Marcus scratched the back of his neck, a look on his face like he was having to admit to a neighbor that he hit a baseball through their window, even though none of it was his fault. "These pipes broke, and before we could get the water to them turned off, it kind of sprouted into the air right toward the 220 volt outlet for the cook top—which was also delivered today. We had plugged in the cook top to make sure it worked, but the plug wasn't in all the way and, well, it got fried."

Joselyn ran her hands over her face. One little stumble by one person, and this much damage had dominoed its way through their shop. Marcus stepped up next to her and put his big, strong arms around her and she leaned into him, soaking in what comfort she could take.

Then, before she had even felt his arm around her long enough to slow her breathing, her phone rang, and she shifted out of his hug to answer.

After saying hello, she just listened as the very apologetic man from the sign company said that they were packing up the With a Cherry on Top sign they had made for the outside of the building, and it had been dropped and couldn't be repaired. They were going to have to start over and make a new one, and although they were going to try, they couldn't guarantee that it would make it before opening day.

In a calm voice that sounded eerie even to her own ears, Joselyn thanked the man, hung up the phone, and then said, "The Main Street Business Alliance meeting started four minutes ago. We better get over there. And we might be minus an outdoor sign on opening day, too."

The events this week kept taking swings at Joselyn's confidence in being able to run a business, and they seemed to hit each time they swung. And now she and Marcus were about to step into a room filled with successful business owners. She had hoped that they would be able to slip in to the back, unnoticed, especially since they were late.

But the moment they walked through the door, the elderly Ed and Linda Keetch were at the front, conducting the meeting, and saw them immediately.

"It's the couple of the hour!" Ed Keetch called out.

"Everyone," Linda said, "I would like to introduce you to Nestled Hollow's newest business owners on Main Street. No, no, no, don't sit down. Come right up here to the front so we can all say hello."

Joselyn's cheeks burned as they went up to the front, and she gave a little wave.

"I'm sure we probably all know you," Ed said, "but in case anyone doesn't, tell us your names and about your business."

Joselyn looked out at the crowd of a couple dozen people, all of whom she had great respect for, and her mouth went dry. She had never felt like such an imposter in her life. She didn't belong up here.

Luckily Marcus knew her well enough to interpret the look on her face, so he talked for them. "I'm Marcus Williams and this is Joselyn Zimmerman. We are leasing the old hardware shop. Nate Elsmore is doing construction on it now, and we plan to have the grand opening of our ice cream shop, With a Cherry on Top two weeks from Saturday."

Whatever unstable look she wore on her face must've been visible to everyone, based on the looks of question and pity they were throwing her direction. She felt like she should say something, or somehow get rid of this expression on her face, or at the very least, run. But thank the heavens for people with hearts like the Keetchs, because they seemed to get what to do.

"Two weeks," Linda exclaimed. "Ed, remember everything that went wrong at Keetchs Burgers and Shakes two weeks before we opened?"

Ed took a few steps toward Linda and wrapped one of her wrinkled hands in two of his. "Only the parts I didn't successfully repress." Everyone in the room chuckled. "Of course, those parts could still fill a book."

The Keetchs always seemed to know what to do, but Joselyn seriously doubted that they had as many struggles as Ed made it sound. Even though she knew he was likely embellishing by leaps and bounds, it still made her heart calm down a little, and she felt like she successfully relaxed her face a teeny bit.

"Those were definitely some tough times. We were young, like you two, and made so many mistakes." Linda looked at Ed with such fondness that it made her wonder if they had figured out all their relationship stuff long before they tried to create a business together. "Well, we all plan to give With a Cherry on Top the kind of welcome Nestled Hollow is famous for. Ed and I will get with you over the next week to see what you need and finalize the plan, then we'll discuss it more at next week's meeting."

That entire discussion was supposed to take place at this meeting. With as frazzled as she was, she was grateful that Linda recognized how bad that would be right now. She and Marcus took seats in two of the empty chairs, and the meeting continued in the way Joselyn guessed it usually did—by planning ways to celebrate with the town and to bring in tourists.

As she sat in this room full of success stories, sitting next to Marcus, she couldn't help but wonder if this partnership was ill-fated. So many things had gone wrong this week, culminating in a firestorm of things going wrong. That couldn't be normal, and it couldn't be coincidence. Maybe it was a sign that joining as partners was a bad idea.

After all, she'd had reservations about it from the very start. Her family had reservations. Maybe she and Marcus should've listened to all those warnings instead of being so blinded by excitement for their business. Her family loved both her and Marcus, so if they were warning against being a partnership, in business or romantically, it was for a reason.

The first day Marcus had asked her to be his consultant, she had told him it was a colossally bad idea. She had known back then. Maybe now that she was finally seeing around the excitement to see that it actually was every bit as colossally bad of an idea as she had feared, she shouldn't keep going blindly forward.

Tomorrow was supposed to be her last day at work. Maybe it wasn't too late for her to tell them that it was a mistake, and see if they would let her stay.

Chapter Fourteen

Kleinman Terrace closed at eleven on Friday nights, but just like most Friday nights, tonight they had a sharp slowdown at nine p.m. Just like he usually did when the orders slowed, Marcus started cleaning up his area in the kitchen from the commotion of a very busy night, and preparing for the last orders that would trickle in until closing time.

And trying not to think of Joselyn and how things had been feeling off about them, or about the way things had been feeling off about the entire Zimmerman family since they told them that he and Joselyn were business partners. Nate had texted them both to give an update on repairing the damages to the building and where they stood in the time line, and Joselyn had responded to the text thanking him. That was the only text he had gotten from her all day. Over the past ten weeks, he didn't think he had gone a day without fewer than a dozen texts from her.

In the midst of the cacophony of thoughts in his head, he had barely noticed that the kitchen had gotten quieter than it ever was when the restaurant was open. He was just wiping down the stainless steel counter when he heard singing coming from the door to the front lobby and turned. His sous chef, line cooks, prep cooks, soup and sauce cook, bartender dishwasher, most of the servers, and the two owners were all filing through the door, holding a giant cake, and singing *For He's a Jolly Good Fellow.*

Warmth spread through his chest as he watched his co-workers—his friends—all gather around him and the head server place the cake on a stainless steel rolling cart right in the middle of the circle they were making.

"Wow. I am touched. I want to wrap you all in a giant bear hug!" There were too many people for one bear hug, of course, so he started shaking hands and clapping people on the backs while a few people passed out champagne glasses and someone filled them with sparkling cider—the Kleinman brothers had a very strict *No drinking while at work* rule.

Once everyone had a glass in their hand, Kade Kleinman said, "To Marcus, who is on to exciting new things, but who will always be remembered as one of the best—and friendliest—Executive Chefs we've had."

He held his glass out, and everyone shouted, "To Marcus!" and clinked glasses.

Max Kleinman held out his glass toward Marcus. "For a lot of reasons, we're sure going to miss you around here. Well, all of us except maybe Dustin."

Everyone laughed as Marcus put on his best hurt expression and turned toward Dustin.

"Oh, I'm going to miss you plenty, buddy, and I plan to frequent your ice cream establishment often. They've just softened the blow of you leaving by naming me your replacement."

"That's fantastic!" Marcus sat down his cup and wrapped his arms around his friend, then pulled back and shook his hand. "You'll do great. This kitchen will run well when I'm gone." He turned to the rest of the group. "Did someone open the back door? I think I might've gotten some dust in my eye." To the laughs of the group, he pretended to wipe away a tear. In truth, though, he was actually getting choked up at the thought of leaving everyone here.

A few people had to rush out to take care of customers as someone cut the cake and they passed it out, and more and more people said a goodbye and headed back to work. Once they were gone, Marcus headed back to his work station and wiped down things a bit better as he glanced to see if more orders had come in.

Dustin stood next to him, leaning against his counter. "So are you having second thoughts about the new business, or are you just sad to leave us?"

Marcus looked up from straightening the bottles of olive oils and vinegars.

"I mean don't get me wrong—you looked like you really enjoyed that sendoff. But when we weren't distracting you with that, you've seem pretty down."

No orders had come through, so instead of trying to find something to occupy his hands, he just turned around and leaned against the counter next to Dustin. "You know that, beyond a couple of cousins who don't live near, the Zimmermans are my only family." He shrugged a shoulder. "Maybe I shouldn't have asked Joselyn to be my business partner. Maybe I shouldn't have started dating her. It had just felt so right! But now it feels like they're pulling away. I'm afraid that if I'm not careful, I'm going to lose them all."

"Is there evidence? Or is this all in your head?"

It was hard to explain the distance he was feeling from the Zimmermans. It was just something he recognized after being a quasi-member of their family for the past nineteen years. So he stuck with the facts. "Everett stayed quiet about me asking Joselyn to be my business partner for a full week. Last Saturday when I was moving into his basement, he let me have it. He made me promise as a teen to never date her. I broke that promise then, and I broke it again now."

"He'll forgive you."

Marcus shook his head. "He said what he was most hurt about was that, as my best friend, I didn't even go to him when I was thinking of asking Joselyn to be my partner. That he found out almost a week after the fact, and only when we told everyone else." He winced at the memory. "So I decided that I would give him a heads-up about me and Joselyn dating, too, since we hadn't told the rest of the family yet."

Looking back, that hadn't been the best time to add one more thing for Everett to be upset about him not sharing. Another thing he hadn't shared with him was that when he was downstairs in his bedroom and Everett and Hannah were in their living room reading and chatting before bed, he could hear them through his vent. Not that he was home every night in time to hear them, but the two nights he was, he could hear Everett still working through his feelings of betrayal at being left in the dark and worry for what it might mean for their family, along with Hannah's attempts at convincing him it would all be okay.

At the sound of the order printer, Dustin twisted around and grabbed the slip of paper from the machine. "You've been in love with Joselyn since well before I met you. If you ask me, I say you forget about the family and you two do your thing and not worry about what they think."

Marcus shook his head. It wasn't just about him giving up the family he loved. It wasn't that would mean giving up his best friend. "This family isn't like yours. I couldn't do that to Joselyn."

Dustin handed him the slip of paper containing the order he needed to prepare. "It sounds like you have a lot of thinking to do, then. Good luck, buddy."

It wasn't just the family thing that was worrying him. So many things had been going wrong with the business that he was sure that Joselyn was wishing she had never partnered with him. He should've just let her have the building from the beginning, and they probably wouldn't have had so many troubles.

When Marcus pulled up to the shop Saturday morning to meet with Nate, Joselyn was already getting out of her car. He met her on the sidewalk and gave her a quick kiss, but he could tell that she was every bit as stressed out as he was. Her motions were quick and focused on the building, and her eyebrows were scrunched together like they always were when she was worried or thinking hard.

Once they walked inside, they found Nate and one of his crew working on installing the tile flooring back in the kitchen. There was still evidence of the damage the ice cream machine caused Thursday afternoon, but for only being a day and a half later, it was looking much better.

"Come on up front," Nate said, getting to his feet. "I've only got one guy here today because my crew doesn't work on Saturdays, but we're trying to get everything ready in plenty of time for you to decorate and get everything in place and have time to make the ice cream before opening day."

Nate had been focused on business, but possibly because of their lack of enthusiasm, Nate threw out a jauntier, "Just two weeks away from the big day, right?"

Marcus tried to force a smile through his worries about the place. "Yep!"

"Okay, well," Nate said, "I asked you two to come in today because I contacted the guys who did the counter top, and they can't replace it with the same materials because they won't be back in stock in time. So we have these two choices instead, and I think either one would look good with your color scheme. What do you think?"

One was wood strips that looked nice, and would look just great—it was a beautiful color—but it reminded him too much of a chopping block at the restaurant, and didn't make him think "ice cream" at all. The other was a nice, crisp white, which really went well with the other white accents they were using. So he pointed at the white sample at the same time Joselyn pointed at the wood one.

Joselyn stiffened for a small moment, so Marcus said, "Actually, let's go with the wood." But Joselyn had also immediately said, "White's just fine. Let's use it."

Nate looked at them like he was amused, but quickly tried to hide it. Probably because both Marcus and Joselyn were so on edge.

"The wood countertop," Marcus said, a bit more firmly.

"This is Sandra," Joselyn said, lifting her phone so she could see the screen. "We should probably take this."

Nate gave them a nod and headed back into the kitchen area to work on the floor, and Marcus and Joselyn headed toward the back of the shop while Joselyn answered the call and put it on speaker phone.

"Couple of bumps, sweeties," Sandra said. "Nate will have the booths ready to upholster by Wednesday, but the fabric we ordered is on back-order. I've already pulled three different fabric samples that I think will work, though, and all three can be delivered by Wednesday."

Joselyn didn't ask about them—she just said, "You said a *couple* of bumps?"

"The other," Sandra said, a bit more cautiously this time, probably sensing Joselyn's mood, "is just that we're a couple of tables short. That one will work itself out, I'm sure. Let's not worry about it. So what do you think about the fabric?"

Joselyn looked at Marcus, so he said, "I'm fine with whatever."

"I am, too. Do you want to just pick the one that will look best?"

"You... don't want to?" Sandra seemed to not know how to respond. "Okay. I'll send a picture of it later."

After Joselyn hung up the phone, she pushed open the back door and headed outside. Marcus followed her into the back parking lot, toward the building that would soon be Macie's Paws and Relax, where the grass between the two buildings was finally free from snow after so many months.

Joselyn slumped her back against the building.

"Rough night?"

She nodded. He wanted to reach out to her, wrap his arms around her and protect her from everything in the world that could possibly cause her to look so downcast. But something about the feeling he was getting from her made him stay a few agonizingly far feet away.

"Remember back two and a half months ago when we started planning this new business?"

He nodded, smiling just thinking about it. If anyone ever asked him to name the most magical part of his life, it would definitely be that.

"We stopped having fun."

He let out a long, slow breath. Dealing with the dozens of problems they had come across in the past week had been anything but fun. He was tired enough that if someone had told him that the past seven days had actually been seven weeks, he'd have believed it. Maybe they just needed some distance from the business. Maybe they should go on a date again like last Saturday. He wondered if they had enough time to fit it in. He was about to open his mouth to ask when Joselyn spoke.

"I don't think our relationship can handle being in business together. It throws a wrench into everything, and now nothing is working out." She looked down at the asphalt, pushing a little stone with the toe of her shoe. "Maybe my family knew what they were talking about when they said we shouldn't date."

Marcus realized that at least a small part of him thought he must have been wrong to worry about the Zimmermans, because hearing it come from Joselyn made that part of him feel like it was crashing to the ground. "You think we should call it quits?" The words felt like punches to the gut. But he had to know.

"Not the business, of course." She looked up and met his eyes. "But I think we should stop dating. Let things go back to when they were working out well."

Marcus's mind flashed back to the past ten years and how hard it had been to be around Joselyn but not be dating her.

Now that they had dated again, he knew exactly what he was missing out on. He knew exactly how much he loved her. The thought of sharing a business with her and not sharing a life with her felt impossible. He couldn't do it. He wouldn't survive it.

He slumped against the wall too. He could feel her eyes on his, but he couldn't turn to meet them. Almost like the words were coming from someone else, he found himself saying, "This business would be so much better if you were the one running the show. All of it."

"You don't want to stay being business partners?" Joselyn's voice came out shallow, hollow.

He wanted to stay being everything. He wanted it all. He wanted Joselyn in his life every day. He wanted to hold her and love her and dream big dreams together and build a life together.

He ignored the pain in his chest, the part of him that wanted to beg her to be by his side—in life and in business. Instead, he forced himself to say, "You'd run this better than I ever could. I can either turn my half over to you, or I can be a silent partner." He cleared his throat and plowed forward. "Either way, I think it would probably be best if I wasn't around. I'd been thinking of going back to Hawaii before I found out about the shop—I think I should probably do that now."

He wanted to slide to the ground and not get up for a very long time. But he pushed himself away from the wall to stand up.

"You're leaving? Just walking away?"

"I have to." He took one glance at her, but didn't want her to see how much it was hurting him to walk away, so he turned and walked toward the opposite alley.

Just before he rounded the corner to head toward the front of the building, she said to his retreating back, "You're going to disappear out of my life, just like you did when I was in high school?"

He stiffened and paused, then kept on walking.

This was not just like high school. Back in high school, he had loved her with everything he had. Now his love for her was unimaginably greater than it had been back then. And back in high school, he'd always figured he would recover from the pain of losing her before long. Now he knew better.

Chapter Fifteen

When Joselyn had left the shop Saturday morning after breaking up with Marcus, she had expected to feel relief. There had been so many fears and doubts and worries piling on top of her since they started dating that she thought for sure ending things with him would blow all of those things clean away from her. That she'd be back to feeling normal.

Instead, an intense sadness and longing and loneliness had moved in its place and had stayed with her all weekend. She hadn't even told Macie that she and Marcus broke up. Her sister would want to grieve with her and then spout wisdom, and Joselyn didn't want either. She had spent the rest of the day Saturday and all day Sunday holed up in her room, furiously attacking her spreadsheets, trying to get things all figured out to the point that relief would come. That everything would fall into place.

But they hadn't. She glanced at her phone—8:13 a.m. on a Monday. If she hadn't had her last day on Friday, she would be pulling into a parking spot at LLE Financial right now, ready to start a new week at work. The fact that she wasn't made so many emotions swirl around inside her that she wasn't even sure whether positive ones or negative ones were winning. She had decided to just ask her boss on Friday straight out if she would be able to come back if things didn't work out, and he had said that they had hired her replacement, but would always have a place for her there.

But for right now, she had a lot of work to do. Their grand opening was a week from Saturday, and if Marcus wasn't going to be helping her right now, she had even more to do.

She just wished he was here doing it with her. Until they started dating, they had worked together so well! He would come around soon and they would get this business going together. He had to. They both had put too much into this business for him to just walk away. They had both grown and changed a lot since high school—he wouldn't just disappear like he did last time. She hadn't been allowing herself to think about him. But when she slipped and did anyway, she thought about how much she missed dating him, too. And how much she missed everything about him.

"No," she told herself, slapping her hands down on to her desk and pushing herself to standing. This was a time for working and planning, not for mourning or wallowing. Macie was gone running some errands for her own business, and she heard the mail carrier's truck outside. She figured it was a good time to take a break, stretch her legs, and grab a few seconds of sunshine.

As she stepped out onto the porch of her and Macie's apartment, she forced herself to take a slow, deep breath of the fresh mountain air, feel the sun on her face, and notice the green blades of grass poking their way up through the brown, the green of a couple of flowers she hadn't known they had—

tulips, maybe—pushing through the dirt by her mailbox, and told herself things would be okay.

She opened the flap to the mailbox and pulled out a few envelopes and a small box just as Hannah turned the corner two houses up, jogging behind her double stroller, Drew and Jason strapped in side-by-side and each holding a stuffed animal. The sight of her, someone who was actually living in the same home as Marcus, made the pang of longing strike deep in her heart. Joselyn waved at her sister-in-law, and Hannah neared, she slowed her stroller to a stop.

Joselyn might not have told Macie that she and Marcus broke up, but based on the look of sorrow that Hannah was giving her, Marcus had definitely told her and Everett.

"How are you?" Hannah asked, like she was talking to an injured animal.

Joselyn shrugged. "How is Marcus?"

"Not well." Hannah turned to glance the direction of their home, as if she could see it from there, or see how Marcus was at that moment. "We haven't seen him outside of the basement too much, but he's gotten most of his things packed up and ready to be shipped."

Panic hit Joselyn like a force and amplified the longing for him. "He's really moving?"

Hannah cocked her head to the side. "To Hawaii. Didn't he tell you?"

"I just didn't think he would. Or that it would be a while from now. That we'd have time—" She stared down at the mail in her hands, even though so many thoughts and feelings were rushing at her that she couldn't take any of it in.

"It'll be soon," Hannah said. "I'm not sure when, but he got an app on his phone for last-minute flights. It'll alert him when one opens up."

She thanked Hannah and headed back into her apartment in a daze, collapsing at their kitchen table, the mail spilling across the surface.

What had she done?

She let her head fall into her hands and stared at the box for a full minute before she noticed its existence enough to be curious about it. After grabbing a pair of scissors from the drawer, she cut the tape and opened the flap. Inside, all stacked so neatly next to each other, were the business cards that she and Marcus had ordered.

She pulled one out and looked at the logo they'd had made with what was now their signature colors, the company name they had come up with that late night in the kitchen at Kleinman Terrace when they were making ice cream, and the picture of the two of them. They had been sitting across the desk from Sandra during their first meeting with her and she had said they were so adorable that she had to grab a picture. She sent it to her and Marcus, and they had loved it so much that when they became partners, they decided to use it for their official business picture.

Joselyn reached out a finger to their picture. Their faces were so full of excitement at the possibilities in front of them, at knowing they were creating a business from scratch that hadn't existed before.

Tears ran silently down her cheeks, dropping onto the table, making the card look blurry in her hands. How had she given up on the two of them as a couple? How could she give up on the dream they had on that day?

She wanted to hear his booming, "Good morning, Sunshine!" greeting every morning. She wanted his strong arms around her. She wanted to work side-by-side with him. She wanted to spend her life dreaming with him and working toward those dreams. She wanted the man who had been part of her family with her siblings and parents for most of her life. She wanted that man to start a family with her. She wanted the man who knew no stranger and gathered everyone in. She wanted the man who, when everyone wanted to be around him, wanted to be with her. She wanted that open, welcoming smile that drew people in. And she wanted that smile that he kept just for her. She wanted the love and support he kept just for her. She wanted it all.

Yet she'd made the worst choice of her entire life and thrown it all away. She dropped her forehead to her folded arms on the table and cried.

Chapter Sixteen

*M*arcus headed into Elsmore Market and made a beeline to the non-foods section in search of shipping boxes. Even though he had moved in to Everett's and Hannah's basement just nine days ago so he knew very well how much stuff he had, the number of shipping boxes he needed to send the things he really wanted to keep still surprised him.

He had thought of taking everything that wasn't logical to send to Hawaii over to a storage unit at Pack It In, but he realized that it was a tether holding him to Nestled Hollow. Proof that he was still holding on, hoping that something would work out between him and Joselyn, and then he could just pull himself back on that tether.

He knew he couldn't go through life like that. His heart wouldn't survive. They had tried dating twice, and it hadn't worked out either time. He had to face that it was time to move on whether he wanted to or not. So he cut that tether, and listed everything for sale online. Ten years ago, their breakup had gutted him. This time, the pain of losing her was so great that he couldn't imagine his heart could possibly ever feel whole again.

The only way he would survive was to move far enough away that she, and the entire Zimmerman family, felt like a distant memory. A dream. Something no longer real. He had dated people over the past ten years, but he hadn't ever been able to convince himself to have a relationship with anyone who wasn't Joselyn, and he couldn't imagine being able to anytime in the future, either. He would just have to learn to be okay with that.

While he was studying the sizes of boxes and mentally putting the items he had left in them, a notification sounded on his phone and he pulled it out of his pocket. It was his last-minute flight finder app, and a one-way flight to Hawaii had just become available. It was leaving tonight at 8:10. He glanced at the clock at the top of his phone. There should be enough time to finish boxing up everything he would have Everett ship to him once he had an address in Hawaii to ship it to, to pack a suitcase, drop off the last items that hadn't sold online yet at a charity, go to the lawyer's office in Denver who was making the business switch over to Joselyn official, and still make it to the airport with plenty of time.

He pressed the "Claim my seat" option and put in all of his information, then touched the "Purchase" button, waited to make sure the email verification showed up, then pushed the phone back into his pocket.

After grabbing the boxes he needed, he headed up toward the front of the store to pay, but Ed and Linda Keetch from the Main Street Business Alliance turned onto his same aisle. Great. He had been hoping, for possibly the first time ever, not to see anyone while he was in the store so he wouldn't have to fake happiness.

"Good morning!" he said, trying to make his voice sound normal and trying to smile big. He wasn't sure if he pulled it off.

"How's the business going?" Ed asked, shaking his hand while clapping him on the back with this other hand.

"It's going."

"I remember those first days of Keetch's Burgers and Fries," he said. "The grand opening went great, but for those few days after, you're not sure if people will actually come. Anyway, we've been meaning to stop by and talk with you. You know—"

"Ed, stop," Linda said, placing a wrinkled hand on his arm, but with all of her focus on Marcus. "Oh. Oh, no. You two already broke up."

Marcus's eyes shot up in surprise. "You knew we were dating? Who told you?" They hadn't even told all of Joselyn's family yet.

"No one told us," she said in a calm, quiet voice. "We just knew by looking at the two of you."

"Starting a business is hard on a relationship," Ed said.

Standing near the end of the non-foods aisle, Marcus really looked at both of them. "How did you two make it through it?"

"Sweetie," Linda said, this time placing her hand on Marcus's arm, "we weren't nearly so daring as to start out a brand new relationship while starting out a brand new business."

Ed chuckled softly. "No. Instead, we decided to start it when we had five kids, all under the age of ten."

"But we'd gotten through a lot of bumps and our relationship was solid. Even though we had, it still taxed us to our max. Don't give up on each other. Things can still work out."

Marcus looked down at the linoleum. "I don't think she

wants things to work out between us. She has made it clear that she's fine with me as a business partner, but not fine with us as a couple."

"Do you know what you want?"

He knew. He wanted to be her partner in everything. He wanted to date her, marry her, have a family with her, grow old with her, wake up every day of his life next to her. He wanted to run With a Cherry on Top beside her. He wanted to walk hand-in-hand with her through all of life. He wanted to be there every time she got that sparkle in her eye and smile on her face with a new idea. He wanted to laugh with her and reminisce with her and make new memories with her.

He nodded.

"Are you sure she knows what she wants?" Linda asked.

He shrugged. "Ever since we first met when I was nine and she was seven, she has seemed to know exactly what she wants and is working toward it."

Ed clapped him on the back. "Don't give up, son. Fear gets even the best of us and works to confuse us into taking the wrong path."

Marcus thanked them and went to the counter to pay for his boxes, and then headed back to Everett's to pack them up. It sounded like they were asking him to have hope, and hope was much too dangerous to even consider having.

Chapter Seventeen

_B_y the time Macie got home that afternoon, it was after four, and Joselyn had managed to stop crying, move from the table to the couch, and stare off into space for hours. Her stomach was growling from not eating, the couch was more comfortable yet not comforting, and staring off into space had given her no answers. Now she just felt numb.

Macie stood in the doorway, bag hanging from her shoulder, keys in hand, looking at Joselyn. After a short pause, she said, "You two broke up."

Joselyn nodded. "I messed everything up, and I don't know how to fix it."

There was a good, long pause before she said, "Don't know how? Or are afraid to?"

Joselyn looked over at her sister.

Macie set her stuff down and joined her on the couch. "Tell me what happened."

She took a deep breath and it hitched at the end from being curled into herself and all the crying. "You know, we got along just fine before we started dating. The parts where it was just the two of us brainstorming and planning and getting things set up—those parts were all so great. Then, I don't know. We just started disagreeing and all the bad things just started happening."

Macie had her legs crossed, facing her, and she reached out and pushed a lock of hair out of Joselyn's face. "Maybe you weren't getting along because you were both tired. Burnt out. You two have worked nonstop for the past few weeks."

"Maybe. But Macie, a lot of things have gone wrong."

"What I'm hearing is that there were a lot of factors outside of your control that didn't go according to plan. It wasn't something either of you did or didn't do."

"Right. It was an omen."

"It wasn't an omen. You don't even believe in omens." After a pause, Macie asked, "Do you love him?"

Joselyn turned to sit cross-legged facing Macie. "I do. So much. I realized that I always have—it just took me a bit to figure it all out. Now I can't even imagine life without him, ever. Being with him just felt..." she searched for the words to explain it, "exactly right. So much more right than anything I've ever guessed something could feel."

Macie was quiet, so Joselyn just looked down, absently playing with the ankle of her sock.

"Do you know what I think? I think that this is all your brain's fault."

Joselyn chuckled and wiped away a tear, shaking her head. "Leave it to a little sister."

Macie chuckled, too. "Really, though, I think your brain is just trying to protect you from any possible dangers from doing something big and scary. It's the same thing it was doing by trying to get you to procrastinate opening your own business—using fear to keep you from taking a risk. It did the same thing in trying to get you to procrastinate having a long-term relationship with anyone. For years, you've been saying that you can't date anyone seriously until you got your life more together.

"Then you started working as Marcus's consultant and doing an amazing job of it. I don't think you could've found anyone who would've been able to honestly say that you didn't have your life together. So then your brain shifted its story and tried to protect you by saying you couldn't date Marcus because you couldn't be successful at a new relationship and a new business at the same time. I want you to think about this logically and honestly and tell me, do you think you need to be protected from a relationship?"

Joselyn lifted a shoulder in a shrug. "He's leaving. I could use protection from that." A flash of how much it had hurt back when he disappeared from her life in high school hit her. It had been the most painful thing she'd ever experienced, and he hadn't even left Nestled Hollow. Now he wanted to leave across an ocean. Permanently. The pain she was facing was unfathomable.

A knock sounded at the door and Joselyn raised up high enough to see the road through the window. "Did you text Mom and Dad?"

Macie shook her head and got up to answer the door. Her parents came inside and walked into the living room, then looked at her with long faces.

"How are you doing, sweetie?" Her mom sat down on her other side and wrapped an arm around her shoulders in a hug. "We were sorry to hear that you and Marcus broke up. We were rooting for you two."

Joselyn looked between her mom and her dad. "You knew we were dating?"

Her mom shook her head. "No. I just found out when I heard that you broke up."

"I know ice cream is the standard break-up food," her dad said, handing her a plastic container, "but given the circumstances, we thought ice cream probably wouldn't help. So we swung by Elsmore's and got you brownies."

Joselyn took the brownies and smiled up at her dad. "Thank you."

He sat down on the coffee table in front of her. "You okay?"

"I don't know. We broke up Saturday morning. Hannah said he's packing his stuff to move to Hawaii soon. I'm sorry I never told you, but Marcus and I also dated back in high school. He disappeared when we broke up then, too. If he's leaving again, then that means he doesn't want to try to work things out. That's what happened last time."

"That's not what happened last time."

Joselyn's eyes flew to her dad's. From the corner of her eye, she saw her mom doing the same.

He took a long, slow breath. "I knew you were dating in high school. I, uh, kind of accidentally caught the two of you kissing by the side of the garage one night. I know you were trying to hide how much you were hurting when you two broke up so we wouldn't know." He shook his head, looking down at the carpet. "But it broke my heart to see my baby hurting so much. With as often as he was always around the house, I knew it would be hard for both of you to recover. So I suggested that he stay away for a couple of months."

"That's why he left?"

Her dad met her eyes then, his full of apology and a pleading for understanding.

It was like someone put a bomb on the spreadsheet page in her mind that had contained hers and Marcus's past, blowing all the cells different directions, and she was left scrambling to gather them up and put them back onto the page in the order they should be in, now that she had all the information.

Another knock sounded on the door, this one more firm and insistent. Macie once again got up to answer it. As soon as she opened the door, Everett came inside, Jason on his hip, his phone in his other hand. Right behind him was Hannah, holding Drew's hand.

"Joselyn, you have to talk Marcus into staying. Oh hey, Mom, Dad. Did you know Joselyn and Marcus were dating?"

Her mom nodded. "We feel terrible that they broke up."

"So wait," Joselyn said, turning back to her parents. "You aren't mad that we were dating?"

"We always knew you eventually would," her mom said. "I mean it's you and Marcus, after all."

"*I* didn't always know," Everett said. "And I was mad."

Hannah patted Everett on the shoulder. "Luckily he has me to talk sense into him. And luckily I'm patient, because it took a while."

Joselyn's eyebrows drew together as she turned to her dad. "But that day at your house, when we found out that we both wanted the same building and Mom suggested we have a business together, you said no."

He held up a finger. "A business partnership isn't the same thing as dating. I know how many disagreements Phillip and I have had over the years in our business. I didn't want a business partnership to impact any chance the two of you had of getting together once you both decided that the timing was right."

Joselyn sat back on the couch, stunned. Had everyone known they would eventually get together but her? Why didn't anyone tell her? Maybe they could've stopped her from making such a stupid choice Saturday morning. And every moment since then.

"And the timing is right for the two of you to get back together. Like *right now*." Joselyn glanced around the room at the sound of Kennon's voice, trying to figure out where it came from. Everett held up his phone, and she saw her brother's face in a video chat. She hadn't realized that he had been there.

"I'm moving back in two months. I've been away from one of my best friends for a very long time—now be a good sister and don't let him leave before I get back, 'kay?"

More knocks sounded at the door, and since Hannah was closest, she opened the door and her brother Oliver, his wife Audra, their five kids, her brother Zach, his wife Lia, their toddler and their baby, and her sister Nicole, her husband Noble, and their four kids all filed into the room, filling every bit of space in hers and Macie's living room.

"What are you guys doing here?" Joselyn asked, bewildered.

Oliver held up his cell phone. "We got the 'All hands on deck' text from Everett." He turned toward Everett. "So what are we doing?"

"We're getting Joselyn and Marcus back together."

"Yes! It's about time!" Oliver high-fived Everett, then turned to Joselyn. "Wait. *Back* together? You two were dating and I missed it?"

Everett looked down at his phone. "Swear word!" he shouted, his go-to curse word whenever their mom was in the room. "Marcus just texted. He said he just arrived at a law office in Denver to sign the business over to Joselyn, and then he's headed across town to the airport. He got a flight that leaves tonight!"

Joselyn flew to her feet, her heart racing, adrenaline spiking. "I have to stop him. I have to tell him I love him." She took two steps toward the door, then turned and took two steps toward the kitchen and her keys, her brain going so many directions at once that she didn't know where to go.

The room erupted in a flurry of action, a kicked-over beehive of twenty-five people in a small area.

"I'll go get the kids buckled in," Everett said, racing out the door.

"Come on, kids," Oliver said, shooing them out the door. "We've got to hurry!"

"Macie," Hannah said, "run upstairs and grab Joselyn something to wear that isn't so..." her hand fluttered Joselyn's direction, "sad. Then Macie, you ride with Zach. Joselyn, grab your makeup bag and a brush, and I'll find you a water bottle. Lia—you're riding in the back of my parents' car."

"Zach," Lia said, passing the baby to him, "go get our kids in the car."

"Joselyn, you're with me and Lia. We're going to attempt to make it look like you didn't just spend all day crying and getting dehydrated. Hurry, people! We have a relationship to save!"

Joselyn had never seen people vacate a house so quickly. As soon as she came out of the bathroom, make-up bag and brush in hand, Macie was standing there with her sky blue blouse—the one she always got compliments on when she wore, and dropped boots she had grabbed to the floor. Joselyn handed the makeup and brush to Lia, pulled off her shirt right where she stood and had the new one on in less than three seconds, then grabbed the boots and raced outside where her dad already had the car pulled into gear.

Then all five cars pulled away, all heading toward Denver, the airport, and the man Joselyn had fallen in love with.

Chapter Eighteen

---

*A*fter Marcus signed the last of the papers that the lawyer had drawn up to turn the business over to Joselyn, the paralegal slid them into a manila envelope. Marcus handed her the stack of papers he wanted to add to it, and the woman slid them in, too, sealed it and said, "We'll get this mailed out to Miss Zimmerman today."

Marcus thanked her and grabbed his luggage, then headed out front and put it in the trunk of the waiting Uber. As the driver made his way through traffic across town, Marcus mentally ran through everything again, making sure he didn't forget anything. He felt like a jerk leaving her to run the business herself with the grand opening just twelve days away, but he also knew that him hanging around wasn't going to be helpful, either. And he knew that Joselyn was more than capable enough to do it on her own—she would've had no problem at all running a business herself if he hadn't put in an offer on the building in the first place.

Still, though, he wanted everything to go as smoothly as possible for her, and he hoped that all the problems she was going to run into had already happened. He told the lawyer he wanted to just sign over his half with no compensation. It wouldn't make up for him leaving her to pick up the slack on everything, but he hoped it would at least help.

Making ice cream wasn't hard—it just took some practice. It was coming up with the perfect flavor combinations and knowing where to get the high-quality ingredients that were going to showcase those flavors best that was difficult. He had included in the packet that the law office was sending Joselyn all of the recipes for the ice cream flavors he had planned to make for the first month they were opened, along with where and how to get the ingredients.

He included instructions on how to make it, too, and he was sure she would be able to figure it out, but he also included a list of people he had worked with before that he thought she might be able to entice to take his job. Good people he thought she would love working with. He had added his notes on which ice cream flavors he had thought of using as their "flavor of the month," too.

After the driver pulled into Denver International and drove him to his gate, he got out, grabbed his luggage, and stood on the sidewalk, taking one last look at Colorado. The sun was low in the sky and covered somewhat by clouds, the air cool enough that most people were wearing jackets, but not cold enough for him to.

He couldn't see much of the city from where he was, but he didn't need to; all of his memories of this place, especially the ones with Joselyn, were burned into his thoughts for life. It used to be that his memories of Joselyn were limited mostly to Nestled Hollow or Mountain Springs, but everything they had done together over the past eleven weeks made everything in Denver colored with her, too.

Hawaii, though, was the one place he had lived that held no memories of Joselyn. The one place he had lived before he met her. He could go there and not see her in everything that surrounded him. The climate, the elevation, and the scenery was about as different from Denver as he could get, so maybe that would help, too.

Still, though, he didn't know if moving there would help. When he had first moved to Denver to go to culinary school, he had longed for Joselyn just as much as when he'd been living in Nestled Hollow. Going somewhere that hadn't held memories of her hadn't helped him get over her at all, so maybe Hawaii wouldn't help either. It didn't matter where he was—he was going to miss her, and he was worried it was going to be more than he could handle. He was going to miss the entire Zimmerman clan, too.

But maybe him moving would help her.

He breathed in the cool mountain air one last time, then turned and walked into the busy airport. This place had been busy every time he had been here, but it still surprised him that it was this busy on a Monday night. He made his way to security and joined the long line of people dragging their luggage as they inched forward.

By the time he had made it halfway to the front of the line, he thought about how good it was that he had gotten to the airport earlier than he had planned. By the time only a handful of people were in front of him, he glanced down at his watch, worried that he would actually be cutting it a bit close on time.

When a TSA agent waved for him to come to his stand, Marcus walked toward the man, his phone opened to his boarding pass, his driver's license in hand, wheeling his luggage behind him with the other. But a strange sound caught his attention, like a summer downpour on a metal roof, and he glanced toward the direction it came from.

Oliver Zimmerman's oldest, ten-year-old Larissa, sprinted around the corner and came to a halt, searching the crowd. He cocked his head, wondering why in the world she would be in the airport, looking like she was running for her life, when she spotted him and yelled, "Stop!" before bending over to put her hands on her knees, panting from her run.

Marcus glanced at the agent, who waved him off to the side, then yelled, "Next!" to the line.

A fraction of a moment later, the sound he now realized was dozens of feet pounding on the floor as they ran turned into a couple dozen people rounding the corner. All Zimmermans.

Did they come all this way to say goodbye?

Then he spotted Joselyn in the group as she walked toward him, separating from her family. Her breathing was quick and her face was flushed from running, pink spread across those beautiful cheeks of hers. Her hair was down and looking almost wind-blown and he was sure she was the most beautiful sight in all the world. He ducked under the fabric strap of the security barrier, dragging his suitcase as he walked in a daze toward her.

She ran the last few steps to close the gap and when she reached him, she put her hands on the side of his face and kissed him on the lips. "Don't go," she whispered, the urgency in her words matching her kiss as she pressed her lips to his again. "Please don't go." Another kiss. "Stay."

He dropped the handle to his suitcase and wrapped his arms around her waist, his driver's license and phone still in his hand.

She kissed him again. "Come back to Nestled Hollow."

He could kiss Joselyn and listen to her pleas to stay all day, but he had to know what it was that she truly wanted. He needed to hear the words. He pushed the phone and license into his pocket, then put his hands on her hips and stepped back to where he could look into her eyes. "Are you saying you want to get back together?"

She looked at him, those green eyes intense and searching and still pleading. "I'm saying that I was so wrong, Marcus. So, so wrong. About so many things. Yes, I want to get back together! I think it took almost losing you to realize exactly how badly I want you in my life and how you are so perfectly exactly who I want to be with every single day of always. I want to build a life with you and a family with you and grow old with you and run With a Cherry on Top with you and every single bit of it."

He searched her eyes, searching for truth, because the words were too sweet, too perfect, too much of what he had wanted for as long as he could remember for him to possibly dare to believe them.

But all he could see in her eyes was love, determination, commitment. "Are you sure this is what you really want?"

"Yes!" She placed another kiss on his lips. "Yes. More sure than I've been of anything in my life."

Her eyes were full of truth. Beautiful truth. Exquisite, perfect, enduring truth. Heart-mending truth.

He let go of her and bent down next to his suitcase, fumbling to open the zipper just enough to pull out the little box he knew was right on top. His fingers found the box and he gently pulled it out. He had bought the ring a few weeks ago, hoping he would get a chance to propose soon—maybe when the shop opened. He knew that had no longer been a possibility, but it had been the one thing that he hadn't been able to let go of when he packed up the rest of his life to move away. Returning the ring felt too much like he would be parting with the last bit of hope he had in him, and he knew doing that could ruin him. Now, he was so grateful he hadn't.

With the box in hand, he got down on one knee, and he heard the collective gasp of all the Zimmermans in front of him and all the people waiting in the airport security line behind him—people he'd forgotten were even there while he'd been in his bubble with Joselyn.

"Joselyn." He laughed, and as the sound carried, he realized how quiet the very busy area had become. "I've actually imagined this moment hundreds of times, and I can't say I ever pictured it in an airport as I was about to move across an ocean. And I never pictured being at the point where I'm down on one knee, ring in hand, without having figured out exactly what I wanted to say."

But as he looked up at her, her dark hair framing that beautiful face that he had memorized and re-memorized so many times over the years, those perfect eyes that held the best of everything, he knew what he wanted to say.

"Joselyn, I've known you since I was nine, and I've been in love with you every day since then. I want to be with you and love you every day for the rest of my life, too. Please say you'll marry me."

"Yes. Yes!" She held out her left hand as he pulled the ring from the box. Her fingers shook slightly, almost like she was impatient as he was for every day of the rest of their lives to begin.

He slid the ring onto her finger, then stood and brought his hands to her face, sliding his fingers into her hair, cradling her head, like it was the most precious thing on earth, because that's exactly what it was. Then he leaned forward and pressed a soft, gentle kiss on her lips. A promise to always be there for her. She kissed her own promise into his lips, and a peace of knowing everything was exactly as it should be washed over him.

A chorus of "Aww!"s sounded from a couple hundred people, reminding him, once again, that they were there. And because he now remembered they were there, he dropped her into a dip and let himself feel his hammering pulse, so near the surface, the electricity coursing through him as he gave her another kiss—a promise for the future he had always wanted but hardly let himself dream of.

This time, the applause was thunderous. He lifted Joselyn upright and wrapped his arms around her, a grin spread across his face that he knew wasn't going to leave anytime soon. They were both flushed as all the Zimmerman family gathered around them, clapping him on the back and giving them hugs and congratulating them. The family that he thought was going to be lost to him forever was welcoming him in. In all the ways he had imagined proposing to Joselyn over the years, he couldn't say he imagined doing it with nearly all of her very large family present. But somehow, that felt exactly right.

Mr. Z shook Marcus's hand with both of his, Marcus's hand sandwiched between his. "Welcome to the family, Son." Mr. Z smiled at him, and Marcus was pretty sure he was tearing up just a bit. "I've waited a long time to be able to say that."

Once everyone had gotten a chance to congratulate them, Everett grabbed his suitcase, and all the Zimmermans headed back out of the airport. Marcus and Joselyn stayed at the back of the group, walking slowly and taking their time. He wrapped his arm around her shoulders, and she leaned in, resting her head against him.

When they got to the vestibule and everyone else was outside, Joselyn turned and wrapped her arms around his waist, stopping him. "The thought of being with you forever, Marcus Williams, is so right. How did we ever manage to wait so long to get back together after high school?"

Marcus ran his fingers down her temple and cheek, then ran his knuckles along her jawline. "Maybe we just needed to wait until it could be forever."

Epilogue

$\mathcal{I}$f anyone a year ago would've asked Joselyn where she thought she'd be today, she might've been hopeful and said that she would be standing outside of her own business on Main Street, basking in unseasonably warm and sunny weather for November 5th. But she never, ever, would've guessed that she would've discovered that the love of her life had been right under her nose the whole time, that she would've gotten married, and that she would now be waiting with what seemed like half the town to find out the gender of the baby they were having.

Marcus stepped up behind Joselyn and wrapped his arms around her, his hands landing on her growing stomach. He wasn't wearing a jacket, yet his arms were still warm against her. "Are you ready to find out where this next adventure is going to lead us?"

They had definitely had plenty of adventures in the past year. They had gone from planning a business to planning a wedding to planning a new home to now, planning to be parents. The business was going well, the wedding was perfect, the finishing touches were being put on the home Nate was building them on her part of the Zimmerman family plot right next to the house he just finished for Kennon and his family, and now they were about to find out if they were going to be parents to a son or a daughter. She tilted her head up toward him. "If it's anything like our other adventures, it'll be perfect."

Marcus gave her a kiss. "Just like you."

Joselyn hadn't often pictured herself being married before she and Marcus started dating, but even if she had, she wasn't sure she could've imagined anything as wonderful as being married to Marcus was. She couldn't believe she had ever doubted that the two of them would work out. All the hard things they had faced together over the past year had made them strong, and she knew that they could face down anything that came their way.

Macie skipped up to them, excitement barely contained. "Are you ready?" The gender reveal party had been her idea, and she had been the one to go with them to their ultrasound appointment to find out the gender so it could be a surprise to Joselyn and Marcus. Between Macie's excitement of the party and Joselyn's and Marcus's excitement at becoming parents, it didn't take long to turn into a party involving With a Cherry on Top, Macie's new business, Paws and Relax, and half the town.

She and Marcus both grinned, and Macie headed down Main Street toward the big, closed-in tent area she had set up a hundred yards away. As she walked down the middle of the street, she had all the family, friends, and townspeople back up toward the sidewalk on one side, or Snowdrift Springs that ran down the middle of the street. When Macie got to the end, she glanced back at them before ducking into the tent. Marcus moved to her side and grabbed hold of her hand and she clutched on tightly, her stomach fluttering.

With a flourish, Macie flung open the tent wall and her dogs Reese and Lola raced out of it and down the aisle made by all the onlookers toward Joselyn and Marcus, each of them clutching in their mouths a corner of a giant pink flag that billowed out behind them.

"We're going to have a girl!" Joselyn shouted.

Marcus wrapped his arms around her and turned them both in a circle. "We are going to have a daughter." He kissed her on the lips. Then, as if his excitement was too much to contain, he turned to the crowds and shouted "We're going to have a daughter!" He ran toward Joselyn's brothers and he and Everett did a jumping chest bump before he did the same with Kennon. Then he threw his arms around each of her siblings and their spouses and her parents, then raced down the line of nieces and nephews, giving fives to each of them as he went. Then he shouted to the crowd again, "We're going to have a daughter!"

Macie, Hannah, the rest of Joselyn's family, and a good portion of their Business Alliance friends—Brooke, Tory, Alete, Cole, the Keetchs, the Treanors, the Elsmores, Joey, Nate —all gathered around to congratulate her and Marcus, and she hugged them and thanked them all.

Whitney, the woman who owned the Nestled Hollow Gazette and had been Marcus's same grade in high school, stepped closer to Joselyn as she took pictures of the event. As she lowered the camera, she said to Joselyn, "He would be exactly this excited whether you found out it was a boy or a girl, wouldn't he?"

Joselyn nodded. "It's one of the things I love about him. I so can't wait to see how he is as a father."

Whitney looked at Marcus's excitement with a wistful yearning that Joselyn had never seen on the woman's face before. It had only been there a moment, though, before she seemed to wipe it away with sheer willpower, and brought the camera back up for more pictures.

As Marcus made his way around the entire length of the crowd and back, he wrapped his arms around Joselyn again and gave her a kiss that immediately turned into a smile.

"So I take it you're excited we're having a girl?"

Marcus laughed that loud, rumbling laugh that she lived for. "It's music to my ears. I guess this means we can start decorating the back room in the shop, and then the nursery at home as soon as we move in."

Then he turned to the crowd and said with a raised voice, "As you might have guessed by that flag, a big scoop of 'Pink Lemonade Stand' is free for everyone today!" He waited for the crowd to finish cheering, and then added, "I made several buckets worth, so make sure you come inside and get yours. Oh, and the blue 'C is for Cookie' flavor is half price until the buckets I made of that are gone."

The crowd roared in laughter, and Joselyn wondered for the hundredth time how much of With a Cherry on Top's success was because of his incredible ice cream, and how much was because they loved the man serving it. He was definitely an easy man to love.

"Shall we?" She reached her hand out and he clasped his in hers, and they headed inside their shop. They had run into a few more problems when doing the last-minute projects before the shop had opened earlier in the year, but every time she walked in, Joselyn was overwhelmed with the feeling of it having turned out exactly right. This place felt like home, and running it with Marcus brought her more joy than she ever thought running her own business would.

Hand-in-hand, they both walked behind the counter, grinned at each other, then together started scooping up cones full of Pink Lemonade Stand for the endless crowd that poured through their doors.

Author's Note:

I hope you've enjoyed reading Joselyn's and Marcus's story! This book kicks off a series of books that all take place in Nestled Hollow—each with women who own businesses on Main Street, and all with swoony romances and fun characters who find their happily ever afters.

Read on for a sneak peek at the first book in the series, *Second Chance on the Corner of Main Street.*

-Meg

Second Chance on the Corner of Main Street

Chapter One

Whitney sat at her desk in the Nestled Hollow Gazette, moving each of the day's articles into their place in the layout. She glanced up at one of the other occupied desks in this three-desk office. "Scott, how is the business spotlight coming?"

"Still working on it," Scott said, not taking his eyes off his computer screen.

"Kara, how close are you on the repaving article?"

"I need three minutes."

The door burst open, and a red-faced third grader ran in, clutching a paper in his hand.

Whitney stood up. "Lincoln— did you run all the way here from school?"

Lincoln bent over, his hands on his knees, panting. Between heaving breaths, he said, "Yep. I had to stay after to finish my math, so I ran to get here at the normal time."

"You don't have to hurry over here so quickly," Whitney said, grabbing a water bottle from their mini fridge and handing it to him. "It's okay if you come later, or even if you have to miss a day."

He handed a paper to Whitney and opened the water bottle, taking a few gulps. "Nope, a junior reporter always meets his deadlines." And then he saluted her, and she saluted him right back.

As Whitney turned, Lincoln grabbed her arm. "Wait. I didn't see what your shirt said today, and it's a new one, right?" Whitney turned back around as Lincoln read it out loud and laughed. "'I'm a superhero dressed as a reporter.' That one's my new favorite."

Whitney grinned. At the beginning of the school year, Lincoln had stopped in every single day for a week, begging to be a "junior reporter" and bring her the articles he wrote during recess at school. She hadn't wanted to squash the dreams of someone so passionate about journalism, so she'd told him yes. She could tell that he tried so hard on his handwriting that she decided to scan his article and print it exactly as he wrote it instead of typing it out like a normal article, and his feature was an instant hit. It had prompted her to talk to the teacher of the journalism class at the middle school, and they started a "journalist for the day" program in their class. Whitney would've killed for the opportunity to have a by-line in elementary school or middle school.

Just as Lincoln was walking out the door, he held it open for Evia, an older woman with extra fluffy hair, as she stepped inside. "Hello, Whitney. I'm just stopping in on my way to market and wanted to tell you that apparently that storm last night blew a giant branch clean off the Amherst's tree. And you know they're both too old to be cleaning up a mess like that. But on my way, I saw a den of Cub Scouts gathering to haul off the mess. I snapped a picture with my phone," she held it out as evidence, "but I don't know how to get the picture off this blasted thing and over to you."

Whitney helped her to email the picture to Whitney's email account and thanked Evia for the story. As Evia was walking out the door, Whitney smiled. She had lived in this town for her entire life, so they'd seen every awkward phase she'd gone through and every mistake she'd made. And she'd had some incredibly awkward phases and made some pretty big mistakes. She didn't pause nearly often enough to think about how far she'd come, and how great it was to have a town who trusted her. When Mr. Annesley had retired and left the newspaper to her, and then died in a car crash that same weekend three years ago, Whitney would've never guessed that so many people would stop in and give her every story idea they had. She was actually successful at publishing a small town newspaper, when most print newspapers in the country were a thing of the past. The Nestled Hollow Gazette succeeded because it kept its focus on showcasing all the people in the town.

Kara clicked her mouse with a flourish of her hand and called out, "Sent!"

At sixteen years old, Kara was the same age now that Whitney was when she first started working at the Gazette. They both made their way to Whitney's desk and Whitney switched over to her email and opened the file. She read as Kara hovered. The article told about all the potholes on Silver Mine Street, and how unsightly it was and how difficult to drive on, and how beautiful it was going to look when finished.

Whitney looked up at the girl and remembered how eager she had been to please Mr. Annesley when she was first learning the business. She hoped when she was training her young staff that she had the same determination to get it right while still showing a kind sparkle in her eye, just like Mr. Annesley'd had.

"What's the lead on this?"

"Fixing the road," Kara said, like it was the only possible answer. Then her brow crinkled and she paused for a moment before Whitney saw her eyes travel up to the big vinyl letters on the wall behind Whitney's desk— *The lead is the people.* "Wait, it's not the road. But how do I make the people the lead on this?"

Whitney lifted one shoulder. "Who does the damaged road affect? Who will construction affect?"

Kara's eyes looked off into the distance, not really focusing on anything. "Elsmore Market is right on that corner. It won't really affect their customers, but they get access to their employee lot from Silver Mine. Mrs. Davenport lives on Silver Mine, and she has a hard enough time pulling out of her driveway onto a regular road. She might need some help. Oh! And there's a whole neighborhood of kids who ride their bikes down that street to get to the elementary school." With each person she mentioned, Kara's smile grew wider, and Whitney's grew wider right along with it. "I've got a lot of people I need to talk to. Can I get you this article after your Main Street Business Alliance meeting?" Kara glanced at the clock on the wall. "Hey, shouldn't you have already left for that?"

Whitney looked up at the clock that read 3:55, and made a sound like a choked hyena. She smoothed down the front of her t-shirt and dark jeans and grabbed her black blazer off the back of her chair, pushing her arms into the sleeves as she walked to the door. "I've got to run."

"My article will be in your email when you get back," Scott called out as she waved and walked out the door.

She rushed down the street to the old library, followed the sidewalk around to the back of the building, and went down the cement stairs to the basement door and hurried inside.

Yes! There was still a seat on the front row. Whitney sat down next to her friend Brooke. There was a time not that long ago where Whitney would've felt pangs of inadequacy sitting next to someone as fashionable and put together as Brooke, but apparently Whitney had come a long way on that front, too. She liked the outfit she'd adopted as her uniform when she became the owner and editor-in-chief of the paper. It honored the old newspaper pun t-shirt and jeans-wearing version of herself, yet gave the impression that maybe she had a clue what she was doing when she'd swapped out the stylish jeans of her teenage years for the darker, nicer looking ones and added the blazer.

"I've got a headline for tomorrow morning's paper," Brooke said. *"The World Ended at,"* she glanced down at her watch, *"three fifty-eight on Thursday."*

Whitney laughed and then rolled her eyes. "Just because you beat me here for the first time in history doesn't mean—"

Brooke held up a finger. "I beat you here for the first time in history *and* you were very nearly late. I'm pretty sure both are signs of the apocalypse."

Tory, a woman sitting in the row behind them who lived in a house next to Whitney's apartment building, leaned forward. "I've got some leads on an article for you. Are you going to be home tonight?"

"Not if I can help it."

The woman chuckled. "Yeah, you're definitely a busy one. Should I just bring it by the newspaper then?"

Whitney nodded. "I'll be there until probably eight."

Whitney turned back to face the front, and Brooke folded her arms, giving Whitney a knowing look. "What?"

Brooke raised an eyebrow. "You know, normal people aren't gone this much. Normal people actually *like* to go home at the end of the day, relax a bit after working so hard."

"My house isn't relaxing; it's *boring.*"

"Because there's no one there, and you're addicted to being around people?"

There were very few people other than Brooke who could pull off a question like that and not sound rude. But it still stung. Whitney just shrugged and didn't answer.

"When was the last time you went on a date?"

"You know I don't date."

"I know I care about my friend who loves people, and want her to be able to go home at night and not be alone. And the only way that's going to happen, my friend, is if you date."

"I don't need to go on a date to not be alone." She spread her arms wide. "I've got this entire town to keep me company." When Brooke opened her mouth to say something more, Whitney added "Shush. The meeting's about to start."

Chapter Two

Eli shielded his eyes as the mid-morning sun shone down on all twenty-two people at the TeamUp training grounds. He switched his headset mic to *on*. "It looks like teams one and three have managed to get their ropes through the bucket handle without touching the bucket. A hearty high five to you both!"

"And now team three has their rope through their bucket handle," Eli's business partner, Ben, said from the other side of the playing field.

Eli chuckled as team four still strategized in a huddle, arms interlocked, heads down in the middle, looking more like a rugby scrum than five tech development and sales team members. "Team four— how you doing over there?"

One head poked up, and he freed an arm long enough to give him a thumbs up.

The three other teams each had a team member at either end of their rope, the bucket swaying in the middle, carrying their bucket of water, or "toxic waste," to the waste site.

When Eli and Ben made their way to each other, watching

the teams' progress, Ben switched off his mic and said, "Shouldn't you have already taken off?"

Eli glanced over at the open grassy space where they'd set up all the inflatable obstacles for arrow tag— the next challenge, and his favorite one to facilitate. Maybe if he just planned to drive late into the night, he could stay here until late afternoon.

"Avert your eyes," Ben said. "You know you can't stay for that." He switched back on his mic. "Whoa! Team four has left their huddle in a burst of energy. Look at that speed! They're catching up!"

Eli and Ben both moved to the edge of the playing field, where four "waste reclamation facilities" stood, each with a six foot wide circle painted on the ground, and in the center of each circle sat an empty bucket on top of a stool. All four teams reached their circles at nearly the same time, their buckets hanging from the middle of the rope strung between at least two players.

"Remember," Eli said, "that circle represents the radiation zone, and that zone goes all the way up to the sky. Don't let any part of your body cross over into the radiation zone, or you lose it."

"Your dad's going in for surgery tomorrow morning, right?" Ben said, covering his mic. "Nestled Hollow is in the center of Colorado so that's like, what, a fifteen-hour drive?"

Eli shook his head and covered his mic. "More like eighteen or nineteen." He adjusted his mic and said, "Teams, have you figured out how to use that second rope to help dump that bucket, since you can't go inside the circle or touch it? Time to get that rope out!"

"So I guess you won't be there before your dad goes into surgery, then," Ben said. "Watch your hands! Don't let it go over the edge of the circle! When do you have to report in at the family business?"

"I have to be in town for a meeting at four o'clock. Cindy, you reached over the circle with that last adjustment! You just lost that hand— you'll have to keep it behind your back from here on out. Team three, she's struggling to keep that bucket from tipping— help her out!"

Eli watched in silence as all teams stood with two members each standing on opposite sides of their circles, the rope stretched between them, the bucket hovering in the middle, near the bucket they needed to dump it into. Two more players from each team were stretching the second rope out between them, and each moving into place.

It was amazing how well StylesTech had improved since the beginning of the week. StylesTech management had sent two departments to TeamUp— sales and development, because they couldn't stop arguing and blaming each other. Eli and Ben had mixed up the teams for each challenge and only two and a half days later, both teams were working together like pros.

Man, he loved his job. It was ridiculous how much he was going to miss it while he was gone.

All four teams guided the second rope to push against the bottom portion of the bucket, while the two team members with the rope through the handle were pulling forward, causing their buckets to tip, pouring the water into the empty bucket on the stool.

"And team four has finished!" Eli called out, while team four celebrated.

"And team two!" Ben said. "Oh! Bad news, two, Frank just cheered a little too close to the radiation and just lost an arm and a leg. Bummer, Frank. Looks like you'll be hopping for a while."

"Team three finished!"

"And team one!"

Eli made a show of putting on an invisible radiation suit, complete with helmet, and went inside each circle to see which teams had managed to get enough of their toxic waste into the reclamation facility.

He stepped out of the last circle, pretended to take off the radiation suit and announced, "All four teams completed the challenge. TeamUp—"

All twenty StylesTech employees shot a fist into the air and yelled, "To triumph!"

Eli glanced over at the dirt parking lot at the edge of the training fields, where his car sat packed with everything he'd need to stay in Nestled Hollow for the next four to six weeks, and sighed.

Ben clapped his hands together. "We've got cold water and Gatorades and fruits and other snacks for you before we head into arrow tag. But first, we've got one more team activity."

Eli's attention shifted to Ben. This wasn't in the schedule. Ben didn't look at him, though; he just kept his eyes on the twenty team members of StylesTech.

"You all know that Eli here isn't going to be here for the rest of the week, because he's got to head to Colorado. You're all so much fun, though, that Eli doesn't want to leave. What do you think, StylesTech? Can you TeamUp to get him to his car?"

Eli laughed a big hearty laugh as they swarmed him, lifted him up in the air, and carried him to his car, setting him down by his car door.

"Well, that was a first." Eli laughed again. "You all really are rock stars. Remember that first challenge where you were supposed to lead the blindfolded person through the mine field of plastic cups filled with water, but instead you led the blindfolded to step right on every one? And now, not even midday on Wednesday, and you all pretty much just saved the world from an apocalypse with that Toxic Waste challenge. I think I got a little dust in my eye." He wiped his eye like he was wiping away a tear, and everyone laughed.

Ben motioned like he was pushing them all away. "Now get on over to the snack table and hydrate, everyone!"

Eli glanced at Ben and then shook his head, smiling, as he turned off his mic and removed his headset, handing it to Ben.

Ben took off his, too. "You know I've got your back. Or, I guess I'm good at instructing other people to have your back. Now stop worrying about heading home. It can't be that bad. And hey— maybe you'll even meet a girl while you're there."

Eli thought of the one girl he'd ever fallen in love with and the look on her face when he'd driven away from Nestled Hollow twelve years ago. "Ha. Not likely."

"Oh, come on," Ben said, laughing. "You'll be there a month and a half. Maybe you can up your longest relationship record from two weeks to, I don't know, maybe even three." He paused a moment, then in a more serious voice, said, "Going home is always hard. Especially when you haven't been there in twelve years."

Eli glanced west— the direction of home— and took a deep breath. "Yes it is. Especially when you and your business partner were ready to implement a plan to grow the business."

"Don't worry," Ben said, clapping him on the back. "I'll hold down the fort while you're gone. Once you're back, we'll put the plan into play as if you'd never left."

In an effort to drown out any thoughts about where he was headed and what might happen when he got there, Eli blasted music from the moment he got on the freeway in Sacramento until late that night when he stopped at a hotel in downtown Salt Lake City. He was on the road again before eight in the morning, and the music did a good job of drowning his thoughts for the first six hours. But the closer he got to his childhood home, and the more he got texts from his mom saying that his dad's ankle surgery had gone well and that he was recovering in the hospital, the more his mind went to the town that didn't love him, the dad he could never please, and the girl he'd left behind all those years ago.

The road wound between two mountains, and as soon as he came around the last bend, Nestled Hollow came into view, in a small valley with the freeway on one side and mountains forming the other three sides, the lake sparkling in the sunlight at one end, and his childhood came rushing back at him. This view had been forever burned into his memory, but seeing it again in person— as a thirty-year-old now— was different. He exited the freeway and made his way through town, memories hitting him one after another at a rapid pace, flooding his mind with every turn.

He turned on to Main Street, with its creek running right down the middle of the street, separating one side of the road from the other, and drove past Treanor Outdoor Rentals, the family business that was his to run for the next four to six weeks. The place brought back surprisingly happy memories — as a kid he had dreamed of one day growing up and running the family business. He'd loved Treanor's. There was no way he'd choose to run it now, unless his dad wasn't in the picture.

He drove to the end of the second block, just past the clock tower that straddled Snowdrift Springs, did a U-turn at the bridge covering the creek, then found a parking spot right near the library. As soon as he opened his door, he took a deep breath of the crisp mountain air that carried with it the faint scent of pine trees and fresh lakes and good, fertile dirt. As much as he didn't want to be here, he had sure missed that scent.

Eli glanced down at his watch as he walked toward the back of the building— 4:09. Perfect. He figured if he stepped in after the meeting started, it would minimize having to talk to everyone before he was ready. He walked into the downstairs meeting hall. About twenty-five people filled the space, and although there were a few empty seats still, every seat in the back row had been taken. Instead of interrupting the meeting by squeezing in somewhere in the middle, he leaned against the wall at the back.

Eli's dad had brought him to these meetings every week from about age ten until age seventeen, when Eli's parents separated and he started rebelling against everything his dad wanted him to do. He smiled to see that, even after all these years, Ed and Linda Keetch were still running the Main Street Business Alliance. She was talking about the plans for Fall Market, and which Main Street businesses were helping out with what.

And that's when he saw Whitney sitting in the front row and his breath caught in his throat. Every time he'd thought of her over the past twelve years— and he was embarrassed to admit how frequently that was— he had always pictured her still here in town. But he hadn't dared to hope that she was actually still here.

Her hair was shorter— it brushed her shoulders now, but still had big curls and was the same rich auburn color he'd recognize anywhere. He hadn't seen her in twelve years, yet being in the same room with her still caused a fire to burn in his chest and made him no longer able to think straight. Maybe, hopefully, she would turn enough that he could get a glimpse of her face.

Linda glanced down at her clipboard. "I've already made a few assignments— the plans that Joey's Pizza and Subs and Paws and Relax have to bring in tourists really seem to be coming together so nicely. Let's move on to the decorations for Main Street," she said. "The snow pack for this winter is predicted to be the lowest we've seen in a couple of decades, so things are going to get tight for all of us when it comes to the bottom line. We need this Fall Market to be better attended than ever before to make up the difference in revenue we can expect at each of our businesses this winter. So things are going to need to be truly spectacular this year. Next in line for their turn at decorations are the Nestled Hollow Gazette and Treanor's Outdoor Rentals."

Eli stood up straight, feeling like he'd just been hit by an explosion. He hadn't even been in town five minutes, and already he was getting assigned to be on a committee. And heaven help him if Whitney was here with the Gazette. That's where she'd worked back in high school, but hopefully she'd changed professions. He couldn't be teamed up with her, not after being gone for so long. He wondered if she was still angry about the way he'd left all those years ago.

Whitney's hand shot into the air. "Maybe we should switch

that assignment to someone other than Treanor's. Robert will be out of commission until well after Fall Market."

"It'll be just fine, dear." Linda met Eli's eyes and gave a nod. "Robert's son is here to run the store in his absence. He can partner with you for the decorations."

Whitney whipped around in her seat, confusion on her face, until her eyes met Eli's. Then her expression changed.

Yep. She was still angry.

If you'd like to keep reading Whitney and Eli's story, you can get it here.

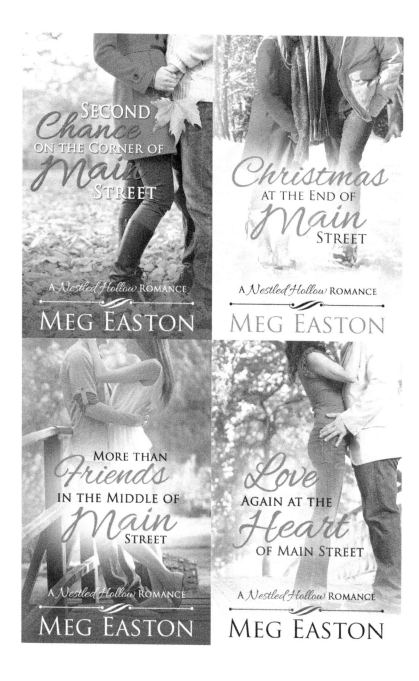

SECOND *Chance* ON THE CORNER OF *Main* STREET

A Nestled Hollow ROMANCE

MEG EASTON

Christmas AT THE END OF *Main* STREET

A Nestled Hollow ROMANCE

MEG EASTON

MORE THAN *Friends* IN THE MIDDLE OF *Main* STREET

A Nestled Hollow ROMANCE

MEG EASTON

Love AGAIN AT THE *Heart* OF MAIN STREET

A Nestled Hollow ROMANCE

MEG EASTON

COMING NEXT: NESTLED HOLLOW ROMANCE BOOK 5

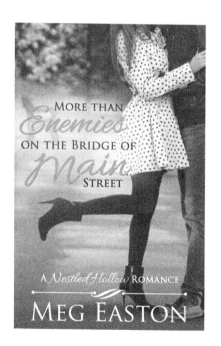

ABOUT MEG

Meg Easton writes contemporary and inspirational romance. She lives at the foot of a mountain with her name on it (or at least one letter of her name) in Utah. She loves gardening, bike riding, baking, swimming before the sun rises, and spending time with her husband and three kids.

She can be found online at www.megeaston.com, where you can sign up to receive her newsletter and stay up to date with new releases, get exclusive bonus content, and more.

If you liked this book please leave a review. Your review can help other readers find books they might fall in love with.

facebook.com/MegEastonBooks

Made in the USA
Monee, IL
11 July 2020